Blood Lake
and Other Stories

Jim Krusoe

Boaz Publishing Company

Address all inquiries to:
Boaz Publishing Company
PO Box 6582
Albany, CA 94706
(510) 525-9459

Cover design by Elizabeth Vahlsing

A hard cover edition of this book was published in 1997

Manufactured in United States of America
ISBN 0-9651879-6-9

CONTENTS

FOR KAITLIN AND HENRY

ACKNOWLEDGMENTS

Special thanks to Lee Montgomery, Judy Bloch,
Elizabeth Vahlsing and Tom Southern.

BLOOD LAKE

and Other Stories

REMORSE

People, and here I guess I mean my lawyers and the parole board, have been talking a lot lately about "remorse," but what they don't seem to understand is, while I agree, yes, it's too bad about my so-called crimes, and yes, I wish things had turned out differently, my feeling remorseful or not remorseful won't change what happened even a little bit. Not only that (and I'm definitely not trying to escape blame by bringing this up), it's clear, at least to me, that this whole affair— the so-called crime spree, the chopper crash (which, by the way, has since been shown to be the fault of shoddy maintenance), the hostages, the shootout in the frozen yogurt parlor—all that could have been avoided if only that highway patrolman, to whom I was demonstrating how if he kept his holster unsnapped anyone could walk right up and take his pistol away, had just had a better sense of humor.

But that's only for the record.

Before all that I was a licensed pharmacist, a man given over to weighing and measuring the quantities of things, because in the stories of my trade the difference between a gram or two is the difference between life and death itself. More than once, even after I had weighed and re-weighed pills and liquids, powders and capsules, still I would be struck by a moment's doubt, and so, as an unsuspecting patron walked out the door or was about to enter a cab, or stood on the threshold of his or her own home, there I'd be, out of breath and shouting, "Wait! Let me check that prescription one last time!" Then how surprised they'd be as I whipped out my portable scale, set it on a front porch swing, or on the roof of their taxi or on the hood of my blue Buick station wagon, and re-measured their prescription just to be sure. Although most often there was no problem at all, still, the net result of such behavior seemed to be a deepening mistrust by the patrons of Yours Truly.

Even so, I was glad to be on the safe side, and those customers who remained afforded me a comfortable living, or at least enough to provide reasonable access to the quantities of morphine I needed to support my moderate habit.

I first began my addiction, as so many others have, one day in the second grade after being passed a marijuana cigarette through the chain-link fence of my schoolyard by a local drug pusher as I was standing around waiting for my turn at kickball. The next day he was back. "Here kid, try this," he said, and handed me a needle along with a pamphlet designed to acquaint the novice diabetic with the basics of self-injection, supplemented by a few of his own scribbled illustrations on how to find a suitable vein and tie off. I walked over to a quiet part of the playground near the life-size concrete hippopotamus a first-grader, Marty, had fallen off only the week before, fracturing his skull. I followed the instructions and injected the drug. The effect was like nothing I had ever experienced. Until that time, the closest I had come was once, when watching a popular television show called *Sesame Street*, I'd held my breath to the point of blacking out. In my last moments of consciousness, however, I was convinced I was on the television, and could see one of the show's characters, a large bird, staring straight into my eyes, saying, "Big guy, seize the day."

Fortunately, in part because the smallness of my body did not require large quantities of the drug, I was able to support my morphine addiction throughout most of my elementary school years by using the lunch money I'd been given (for some reason, my parents believed me when I told them the cost had gone up to $14.95 a day). Later, in high school, I supplemented my income with an after-school job and by selling small amounts of "M," as I called it, at a healthy profit to my friends. By the time I was in tenth grade I knew two things:

first, that I wished to continue taking morphine for the rest of my life, and second, that I should find a way to do it legally.

The moment I decided to be a pharmacist I removed the various psychedelic posters lit with black light I had plastered all over my bedroom walls and replaced them with travel posters of Germany and Switzerland. My grades improved; my parents were thrilled. I entered the college of my choice and obtained a degree. With the generous financial aid of my parents I was able to open a small drugstore, and life rolled along for the next twenty years as if on bearings made of stainless steel.

But, as we all know, change is inevitable. For me, oddly enough, the first change occurred one afternoon while getting a haircut and watching a nature special about gorillas (my barber had a television in front of his chair and was partial, I noticed, to nature specials and to economic forecasts—a far cry from the *Field and Stream*s and *True Detective*s of my youth). There, as the special progressed, even through the imperfect medium of video, I found myself, between glimpses in the mirror, looking into the eyes of one particular animal, a silver-backed male named Samson, as he ripped apart some arm-size stalks of fresh bamboo. Suddenly I experienced a wave of comradeship that I had never felt before. Samson's eyes, for lack of a better way to say it, revealed the existence of a soul without a human mask to hide behind. I was speechless and my eyes filled with tears. "Tony," I said, as he kept raising my sideburns in an effort to get them even (his only flaw as a barber), "one day I will have to go to Africa to see for myself these magnificent creatures in their native habitat."

Subsequent events, of course, have made that dream impossible, but before I knew that, I found myself spending weekends at the zoo, at the gorilla cage, watching these beautiful animals and in particular, one light brown female by the name of Kiki.

Kiki was smallish for a gorilla and had a certain *soignée* quality that the other females, four in number, seemed to lack. Her hair, though dulled by the dust and dirt of the compound, seemed somehow more vibrant than that of her companions, and her forehead, although it may have been my imagination, appeared a touch less low. She had a scar along one thigh (the result of a trapper's cruelty, I found out later) but what struck me most was not her physical characteristics but her social ones. She had a way of standing off to the side of any group— say of her fellow females—and watching them as they signaled the crowd to throw down pellets of zoo-approved treats. (The zoo sold these treats at exorbitant prices from nearby vending machines as a way to raise more money, even going so far as to hint that except for these snacks the animals might well starve.) Kiki's manner, however, was not as cold or scientific as you might expect. It almost seemed that she yearned to join her peers, but something, perhaps even her peers themselves, held her back. So she stood to the left or the right, watching as if she were weighing the relative worth of the two groups: the crowd of people throwing treats, and those receiving them.

These observations, of course, were not the product of a single afternoon, or even two or three. I had been visiting the zoo on an average of five afternoons a week for several months before one day, late in October, after the crowds had thinned considerably, when Kiki's eyes and mine locked for the first time. Incredible as it may sound, in that moment I was sure she knew I had been watching her. At the same time I understood she had been watching me as well. She lowered her eyes, and for the first time, deliberately and resignedly, walked over to where her sisters were begging for treats, and as if to mock me, joined them. I tried to catch her glance, but although she looked both to my right and to my left, Kiki refused to look at me again.

The following day I noticed she was outside the group once more, but then seeing me, almost to confirm my earlier speculation, she slowly walked over to the others and began to beg. I went so far as to buy a treat (two for a dollar) and tossed it down to her. She caught it and looked up at me, then simply dropped it at her feet.

The next Saturday as I arrived I saw Kiki standing apart from the crowd as usual. Again our eyes met, and again she looked away, but apparently in the week that had passed she had decided she could trust me with her secret. She stayed apart and watched, but this time, if I perceived correctly, there was an ironic cast to her stare when she observed the group I was a part of. Embarrassed, I moved away from my peers.

Within a month the two of us were sharing a private joke, and I could see that she looked forward to my visits as much as I did. Little by little, through a modest bribe to one of the keepers, I began the habit of bringing gifts of illegal (but healthful) portions of yogurt bars and whole wheat muffins. Then, with increasing frequency, I found myself injecting a small amount of morphine into one of these snacks and watching as relief and gratitude for the temporary escape from her captivity flooded her sensitive features.

So bit by bit I became a regular at the zoo. Whenever I arrived Kiki stopped what she was doing—scratching her sides or masticating a piece of banana peel—to walk over to the part of the cage nearest to where I was standing. As our bond developed, I began to take longer lunch hours, shutting the pharmacy from noon to two each day. Our "relationship" became well known among her keepers, and an article, entitled "Gorilla Has Friend in Doc," appeared one weekend in the Sunday paper which, while bringing some extra business for a time, also seemed to be the last straw for several formerly friendly, regular customers.

Then one afternoon, as I lobbed one bran muffin after

another into her waiting hands, the keeper (a pleasant man who had once been a CIA operative and had quit the agency following an operation funding a ruthless South American reactionary army) who I had bribed to let me do this, called me aside. "The zoo," he said, "in order to reduce expenses even further is going to auction off several animals, and I'm sorry to say that Kiki will be among them."

I was stunned and heartbroken of course. I could relocate to a place near whatever zoo bought her, but it wouldn't be easy to sell my pharmacy, and the ensuing inspection of my narcotics inventory might prove troublesome.

I checked with a lawyer to see if such an auction could be blocked, but the answer came back in the negative. "Your only hope," my lawyer said, "is to obtain an animal importation permit, the kind that will allow you to keep large animals on your premises for extended periods of time, and then bid for her yourself."

I can still remember the morning (a Wednesday, about eleven o'clock) I backed the station wagon up to Kiki's cage after first having tossed her four and a half apple-raisin rolls laced with morphine, and saw, as I drove her to her new home, her beatific smile for the first time ever in my rearview mirror. I had specially reinforced my house to prepare for any tantrums she might exhibit, but I need not have bothered. After walking through the front door and showing her her quarters, my first act was to give her a shower, followed by a full-body shampoo and conditioner which left her hair glossy and silken smooth. Kiki seemed pleased with the results and totally at home in her new surroundings. We had a light snack and then retired to our respective rooms for a little private time.

That evening, after a late supper of squash, cabbage and baked potato (Kiki was a vegetarian), I invited her to accompany me to the television room, where I quickly learned she liked shows with action—westerns, car chases, and Disney films about heroic animals being her favorites. To the nature programs that had introduced me to the world of gorillas, she was surprisingly indifferent. That evening at about ten, having had an exciting day, we went to our rooms to sleep.

It was shortly past midnight when I first woke to a soft tap on my door, followed by the muffled click of its handle being turned, and then the quiet squeak of the door being pushed open. I smelled the pleasant aroma of wheat germ and honey, and felt the decided pressure of a large body pressing down the side of the bed next to mine. I breathed a sigh of relief. It was clear, even though I was no specialist in animal behavior, that Kiki had decided to be friends.

I have never claimed, as some I have known, to have had access to a wide variety of sexual experience. I've been fortunate to have been loved in varying degrees by several of the opposite sex, though in truth my addiction has probably been responsible for a certain lack of fervor in that area. But be that as it may, I must state with as much authority as I can possibly bring to the subject that making love with Kiki was an experience few have ever had. First of all, there was something primitive about the act, similar, I imagine, though I have never actually been in an avalanche, to being utterly buried by something so elemental. And yet simultaneously, to stroke that silky fur which covered nearly her entire body (excepting her palms and the soles of her feet) also brought to mind something dazzlingly fresh, an alpine meadow such as those we often see in travel posters of Switzerland, covered with tender spring grass and lit by the sun.

I believed then and still believe that the dream of returning to the simplicity of our first world, that of the animal, is as old as mankind. To look into those eyes (after a while I learned to keep the light on) that see only you, to ride or be ridden without thought of destination or consequence, to hear words and sounds which, because the loved and the lover speak no common language, seem to originate in the labials of the soul, surely that must be love itself. In short, what I experienced with Kiki was an ecstasy I have rarely felt outside the very best moments of drug addiction.

So it went for three glorious years. Each morning I woke, leaving Kiki in bed to catch up on the extra sleep she seemed to require, went to work, filled prescriptions, dispensed laxatives, sold condoms, hawked salves, offered cards of sympathy, and at the end of the day hurried back home to make supper, watch TV, shoot up, and then retire to the special world of our passions. Then, as often happens in stories, particularly love stories, once again in my life something changed.

Even before I met Kiki, I had been in the habit of hosting a weekly poker game, and I saw no reason to alter this tradition following her arrival. The players consisted of four, sometimes five people, and Kiki, after first being afraid to be seen in the presence of so many strangers, eventually incorporated herself into the festivities, going so far as to don an attractive yellow apron and, at a nod from me, to pass among us players carrying a tray full of snacks or crackers spread with cheese dip.

In the bloom of our relationship, I have to say she paid no attention to Ken at all, but one evening, after a minor argument earlier that day, I noticed her brushing against Ken's surprisingly hairy body as she passed by him with her tray. Later that night, as she ran her fingers through the sparse hair of my forearms, she appeared to be thinking of something that concerned her and her alone. In the weeks that followed I began to notice that after she had passed among us during poker games, Ken would often be left with an extra Vienna sausage or Pizza Puff, and once, in a fit of what I mistakenly thought was absentmindedness, she simply put the entire tray in front of him. Ken didn't mind at all.

Finally one week I asked Ken to stay behind after the others had left. "Ken," I said, "I know what's going on between you two, and if you really love each other I want you to know I won't stand in your way. But there is one thing you should realize. Through no fault of her own, Kiki is by now a hopeless morphine addict, and should you try to support her habit on your modest salary the only result will be unhappiness."

"I know that, Jim," Ken said. "And I also know who's responsible for the monkey on her back." He looked at me disdainfully. "My advice," he said, "is that you go cold turkey and kick the habit, because that's what Kiki and I plan to do."

During this conversation I was sorry to see a crack appear in the doorway to the kitchen where Kiki, who was supposed to be drying a few plates, had obviously been listening. Ken raised his voice in that ostentatious way people do when they know they are being overheard. "We've talked it over," he said, "and if you try to stop us we'll report you to the law. I love her," he added in the direction of the kitchen door, "and we're leaving."

Suddenly the door swung open and Kiki appeared, carrying a small cardboard box into which she had crammed a few of her personal belongings, including a stuffed opossum I had bought from a taxidermist's closeout sale the first week she had been here. Ken glared at me and Kiki would not meet my gaze, but together they climbed into his fully restored 1957 Chevy Bel-Aire and drove off into the night.

Cold turkey, as you probably know, is a therapy for drug dependence supported mostly by people who themselves have not been addicts. I had tried it once, halfheartedly, and knew its pitfalls. Ken, alas, did not. They apparently began the treatment the following day, and within twenty-four hours Ken was dead, killed by an armoire he had pushed in front of the door to her room as Kiki tried to make her way back to me. Kiki, who never did have a good sense of direction, took a wrong turn and, instead of finding herself safe with me, made the terrible mistake of entering a parking garage, where, unable to find the exit, she was killed by an off-duty highway patrolman.

Who can trace the beginnings of all things great and small? If the first human act recorded in the Bible was embarrassment, then wasn't the second (with several dull years between omitted) that of Cain bashing in his brother's head? According to some, violence is a seed that, when planted early in life, must eventually come to fruition. William Blake describes it as a toxic tree, which, with a little tending, can be lethal. Yet there are those who, to put it simply, don't seem to have a green thumb, those whose natures are so completely benign that no matter what is done to them, they never fight back. On the other hand, however, I suppose for every one of those, there are others who, after a life drenched in the milk of human kindness, suddenly become irritable, have had enough, won't take it anymore, go to a gun store, climb up on a rooftop, bring plenty of food, water, ammo, and start blasting. Oddly enough, I still am not certain to which of these groups I belong.

My recovery from the loss of Kiki was slow but steady. I joined a chapter of Survivors Anonymous, and while I was forced to conceal the exact nature of my bereavement, I remember surmounting stage after stage of grief with increasing exhilaration, even, in the little resting space between denial and blame, looking forward to the anticipation of sadness and anger yet to come. I completed the course, stayed around long enough to help others overcome their own crises, then left to find my own personal solace in planting an organic garden which specialized in roots, some of Kiki's favorite foods.

In time life went pretty much back to normal. I measured prescriptions, came home, ate, watched a cop show or a western, injected morphine, sat around in a sort of reverie, and then went to bed. I canceled the weekly poker games, and as I had never been much of a winner, I didn't really miss them. So far as I was concerned I had had the drama of my life, survived it, and all that remained was a fairly pleasant, mostly downhill, denouement. And that would be that.

Or so I thought until that fateful Thursday morning when the highway patrolman (for the record, *not* the one who shot Kiki, or even close) walked into my store to buy a small bottle of Grecian Formula hair color, which happened to be on sale, and a tube of cola-flavored lip balm. We were alone at the time (about 10:30, if I'm not mistaken) and it was when I stepped out from behind the counter to show him where the hair dye was kept (he'd already picked up the Chapstick, and, in retrospect, may have been feeling a bit defensive about his greying hair) that I noticed that the strap to his holster had been left open. Grabbing his pistol, I playfully whirled it around a few times as I had seen in westerns, and was about to admonish him to the effect that, with such a trusting manner as he had just shown, he certainly wouldn't have to worry about living long enough to regain his youth through the fake artistry of hair dye. But before I could mention a word of this, he made a dive for his ankle where, to my surprise, he had strapped a second weapon. Then, to my even greater surprise, he pointed it at me. He was in a state of unusual emotional distress, and so, recognizing that it was necessary to protect myself, I shot first.

Fortunately my grief training experience stood me in good stead. Even as the smell of cordite hung in the air I ran through all seven stages as easily as if I'd been practicing them for years, ending at hope. I strolled over to the body, picked up both the service revolver and the second, smaller one, squeezed the unfired bullets from his belt, removed his wallet, plucked the lip balm from his fingers, emptied the safe and cash register, packed up all the available narcotics, hung a sign on the door that read, "Closed, Gone Fishin'," turned out the lights, locked up, got in the car, and left.

Why did I flee? It was simple: though I certainly never expected to escape punishment for my act, I didn't see why I should just sit around and wait to be shoved in prison. And as San Francisco had always been one of my favorite cities, I thought it would be nice to visit one last time, then see how far north I could get.

It must be a cliché of the public imagination, (I know it was of mine before I began my "run for it") that escapes of this sort are glorious adventures, complete with high-speed chases, screeching around corners, running stop signs, perhaps even firing out one's windows at pursuers' tires.

In fact, that Thursday was a beautiful day for a drive and I rolled down the windows of the same Buick wagon in which Kiki and I used to go for rides. (Kiki, lying in the back, would be covered by a queen-size sheet so as not to alarm other motorists. She considered it a game, although the first time we tried it, possibly fearful of suffocation, she punched a hole through the body of the car straight to the wheel.) Then I turned on the easy-listening music station and began to relax. An hour or so out of town the station faded and I put on one of my favorite tapes, *The 101 Strings Play Music from "Jaws,"* and continued northward. Traffic was light; I had made good time, and as far as I knew the body of the unfortunate patrolman hadn't been discovered. I decided I could afford to stop early at a small motel near the beach, have a seafood dinner, then get a good night's sleep so that I would be fresh for the next day's drive.

I had accomplished two out of three of these when, at shortly after midnight, I was awakened by a soft tap on the door of my motel room. I opened it to see a young woman dressed in a thin negligee, shivering slightly. Her feet were covered only by two fluffy pink slippers, and her voice was trembling, too. Her first words were, "Do you have a gun?"

Not surprisingly, I suspected a trick, but she quickly went on to add, with great emphasis, as if I were a foreigner, that she was staying in the next unit and there was a large, slow rat beneath her window. I went into my room, emerged with the smaller of my two new pistols, and went to take a look. What she had thought was a rat was, in fact, a mother opossum, complete with five clinging babies, apparently unafraid of our presence, searching through a pile of discarded cigarette butts in hopes of a meal of snails.

I reassured my lonely neighbor, returned to bed, and at last sank into a dreamless sleep before I woke, consumed a breakfast of a fresh fruit cup and Belgian waffles, and continued my journey northward.

The weather continued to be perfect as, concluding a tape of *The 101 Strings Play the Bach Cello Sonatas* (I've always had a taste for classical music), I pulled into Fisherman's Wharf in San Francisco and had a delightful lunch of crab salad, sourdough rolls, and a glass of white wine. By evening I was safely lodged in a quaint coastal inn, and it was there, lying in the antique bed, staring at the ten o'clock news, waiting to drowse off into another night of restful slumber, I heard the first announcement of the vanity-ridden patrolman's death and the speculation that I'd been kidnapped by his murderer. I was described as "a mild-mannered, gorilla-loving pharmacist," and the media did not fail to include a photo of Kiki that I'd taken on the day of our second anniversary. Seeing it anew, I was struck that, though she was wearing a party hat and seemed to be happy, still, there lurked a strange melancholy behind those deep-brown eyes, not just attributable to a precocious longing for Ken, but almost as if, through some animal instinct unknown to me, she had already foreseen where all of this would lead.

"Between," as T.S. Eliot once remarked, "the idea and the act falls some kind of shadow," and it's this shadow of doubt I'm talking about right now, even as it's seized every storyteller from time immemorial. Namely: Why am I relating all of this? The parole board, the governor, the courts have spoken, and frankly, the gist of their message is that I'm some kind of heartless person.

Am I? I suppose the reason anyone writes is to find out

that very answer. And so, in the way that a man whose eyes are failing will often have to hold a newspaper farther away, not nearer, in order to read it, people in general and me in particular have made it a practice to copy down the stories of their lives. So far, you say, so good, but then what? After the story is finally down on paper, what's left to say? That X was a leader of men? Y a corrupter of youth? Z a friend to the blind? K a person who rose from humble beginnings through hard work and good luck to become (fill in the blank) before she or he, ummm, died? What an impossibly crude measure for such a complex bundle of neural firings, emotional hangups, inconsistencies, genes, environment, bad upbringing, as we all are. And then, even supposing we are one of the lucky ones who can say, "Ah, ha! That's who I am!" how long before we have to add, "So what?"

The drive through the wine country of northern California was a beautiful one. The sight of those bundles of grapes, staked out and leaning on their poles as patiently as cattle caught by barbed wire during a Montana snowstorm, soothed me. According to the radio, the focus of "the manhunt," as it was now being called, had switched from two men to just one, now described as "armed and dangerous." The slain patrolman was said to have died heroically in a shootout with a suspected drug pusher, and although I could not see it, I supposed that somewhere a television was broadcasting my picture, possibly one I'd left in the store of me emerging from the wading pool I'd bought for Kiki our first summer. I'd taught her to use the camera, and the photo I had in mind turned out well enough to reveal several "tracks" (as I believe addicts refer to those scars from repeated needle use) on my arms that I had thought would be invisible.

Near the Oregon border I stopped at a place that sold furniture carved from myrtle trees. The chairs and tables turned out to be expensive and ugly, but it was there I noticed the hint of a feeling that someone, though I couldn't say who exactly, was watching me. For the first time I understood what people

27

meant when they said, "The weed of crime bears bitter fruit." Or maybe it was "the seed."

Racing northward, I stopped for a lunch of smoked salmon, rice pilaf and a glass of chardonnay at the Rogue River, got gas in Coos Bay, and at Florence took a couple minutes out to visit the famous sea lion cave, a vast grotto situated between the land and ocean where sea lions come each year to breed and fill the air with such a deafening, undifferentiated roaring I became thoroughly unnerved. I decided I had better turn inland for a while under the assumption that, should I be discovered, it was better to have four directions to choose from than three plus water.

I drove through dusk, shaken as I was by the experience of the sound of nature in the raw and also by the news reports which were becoming more strident in their denunciations of Yours Truly. I planned to stop for a quick snack and then drive on through the night in hopes I could at least get to Canada and maybe the Northwoods before they stopped me. Just where I was going I had no idea, but still it seemed important to continue. Finally I pulled into the parking lot of a frozen yogurt parlor outside a town called Tangent, went in and ordered a double dish of vanilla with fresh banana and shredded coconut topping. It was delicious, and the simple act of consuming something sweet and cool seemed to decrease much of the anxiety that had built up earlier that day.

I had nearly finished the last of my "Tropical Delight" when I turned to notice a small crowd gathering around my station wagon, which was parked outside my window. I left my dish on the table and, fearing some leaking hose or slow-smoldering electrical connection, hurried out to join them.

There, peering out from between the two front wheels of the Buick, was an opossum and five babies. Quickly I deduced she must have crawled through the hole Kiki had made in the fender panel and found a bed there for herself and her children beneath a pile of rags.

"Kick it!" one particularly vicious youngster was shouting

as the confused creature retreated farther beneath the body of the car.

"I'll get a stick to knock it out," another shrieked, and hurried off to a dumpster where there was a pile of sticks suitable for just such a purpose.

"Leave her alone," I said, "and get out of here."

But they just stared at me. "We ain't hurting your car," a smirking hulk of a teenager sullenly replied.

"Leave that animal alone," I repeated, and the one who had loped off in search of a stick returned and began poking at the poor mother to dislodge it from behind a wheel.

"Get out of here, mister. You're a stranger, and that ain't your animal," a voice behind me threatened, followed by a chorus of "yeah" and "that's right" from the surly crowd.

"Get away!" I shouted for the third time, but already I could feel a sharp stick thrust in my back as the crowd tried to push me aside in order to attack the hapless mother, who was defending herself and her children as best she could beneath a series of increasingly brutal pokes.

"Stop!" I yelled, and before I realized what had happened the smaller of the unlucky patrolman's two guns was in my hand and had been fired into the air .

"It's him," I heard gasped from the back of the rapidly dispersing crowd, and that was followed by the sound of someone running off, almost certainly to call the sheriff.

What was I to do? I produced the other, more formidable weapon and took aim at one of the retreating hoodlums. I missed, but apparently this was enough to stop several others in their tracks, and these individuals I herded into the confines of the yogurt shop itself. Despite the fact that I had no idea what I was going to do with these people, I observed that no sooner had I collected them than I began instinctively to refer to them, almost against my will, as "my hostages," and, although it's true that I suppose I vaguely thought of the term "bargaining chips" at some time or another, I certainly never got a chance to explore this possibility because even before I could think of some clear plan, the police arrived and were shouting threats of what they would do if I would not release them.

I introduced myself to my captives, explained briefly what had happened to bring me to this moment, and the hostages (BJ, Jennifer, Sabrina and Rex) quickly bonded with me, as is the usual case in these circumstances. I was relieved to know they had been passive onlookers to the opossum incident, and not the actual torturers. As we sat beneath the counter avoiding the lights of the police snipers, we helped ourselves to our choice of yogurt and toppings, and sang to keep up our spirits. "How many roads must a man walk down..." sang BJ, who had a tenor voice of almost professional quality. Jennifer and Sabrina led us in a spirited rendition of the Michael Jackson hit, "We Are the World," and Rex, after an initial bout of shyness, contributed, in a surprising basso, "I Fought the Law and the Law Won," a golden oldie from the sixties which was climaxed by the thud of a nearby helicopter crash.

We stayed under siege and ate yogurt for two days, and although the yogurt took a toll on our digestive systems (fortunately there was a small rest room we could crawl to), it had the unexpected benefit of somehow compensating for the fact that for the first time in nearly forty years I had missed my daily shot of morphine. If only Ken and Kiki had known, I thought, they might be alive today to tell this tale. (Other drug addicts out there, take note.)

At last, about four a.m. on our final night together, I was awakened by a loud flash, the shattering of the yogurt shop's front window, the noise of bullets and, alas, the screams of the four teenagers who, disoriented by the noise and sudden activity, had stood up behind the counter and were gunned down in a hail of police fire. To this day I can remember Sabrina's last words, "Kiss Tippy good-bye" (although I still have no idea who Tippy was), as she lay with her head in a pool of Jamoca Fudge, the result of the yogurt machines themselves having taken several substantial hits.

It was the great South African naturalist and fellow morphine addict Eugene Marais who, in his seminal study of baboons in the wild, described the subjects of his work as "twilight souls," neither fully human nor animal, and indeed one of those visions that is most unshakable for me is the force of Kiki's stare at times, as she would take a minute out from catching fleas to look into my eyes as if she knew I had some secret she could only dimly sense. At the same time, when I looked back at her I could see a vast intelligence that pulled against invisible bonds, a Samson in the hands of his enemies, which strained with all its might to cross some threshold it could not see.

That great German professional genius, Johann Wolfgang von Goethe, once told somebody that the hardest thing was to be half a genius, though come to think of it I don't know how he'd get that information. As for me, if I were given some sort of magic spatula that I could use to separate the good parts of my life from all the rest, I'm not sure that I could tell the difference. Was it good or bad, for instance, that back in the first grade I had tricked the class bully into taking a plain sugar cube instead of the one that contained polio vaccine, and as a result of his contracting that very illness, he not only ceased torturing his classmates but years later became, although I don't believe he remembers me, the warden at the very prison where I'm currently staying?

A recent American president, responsible for a couple hundred thousand deaths in Vietnam and Cambodia, once remarked, "I am not a crook," and now, for the first time, I begin to understand what he meant. Simply put, it is just that artificial labels such as "crook" and "not a crook" exist only in the minds of the people who are applying them. For Nixon, or me for that matter, to just say "I'm sorry" immediately raises the question, "For what?" At what point in the endless chain of cause and effect does one decide to want to change things? Should Nixon have refused to let the press kick him around? If there ever was a choice, it was not ours, but our parents', and by the time we realized that we might do things differently it was already far too late.

I expect my lawyers still may make a couple more appeals, that there will be a stay, and then there won't, but in the end I don't think that anything is going to make much difference. And when I'm strapped down, the tubes in place, the needle lying in my vein like some old memory, I know that I'll see everyone again—BJ and Jennifer and Rex and Sabrina—all reaching down in a human chain to find me, and Rex will say in that young, deep voice of his, "Take my hand," and I will, and suddenly I'll feel myself being pulled upward.

Nor will I be afraid the chain will break because at the very end will be another hand, a massive one, covered with brown hair and smelling of honey-and-wheat-germ shampoo, a hand that's strong enough to stand the strain of all of us, and maybe Ken as well. And even though by then to you, my gentle audience, I'll be just an illusion, still you have to admit, even with illusions, if some are false then others must be true.

BLOOD LAKE

I

It was late morning by the time Marvin and I finally discovered the little rowboat we had hidden in the weeds along shore a year ago, and pushed it off into the sticky, dark waters of Blood Lake. The best time of the day for fishing had already passed, the very early hours before the flies had begun to settle and the lake's surface hadn't yet begun to thicken into what, by afternoon, would be a clotted crust, impossible to penetrate with all but the heaviest lures.

We began by trolling, taking turns rowing while the other fished and bailed. The boat hadn't taken the last year well, and as we began, it seemed that I was scooping about a coffee can of blood out of the bottom every sixty seconds—that, and trying to keep an eye on my line. Later, as the lake began to thicken, things improved, the blood itself filling in the cracks between the boards, even though the clots made the boat harder to row.

I was using a spinner, one of those bullet-shaped lures with a small silver spoon that turned as it was dragged along and a clump of reddish feathers at the rear. Marvin claimed that artificial worms worked every time, but in truth neither of us was having any luck at all. From time to time we'd reel in and dip our lures in a pint bottle of decoagulant Marvin had gotten from his sister, who was a nurse in an intensive care unit. It was around the knots and swivels that most clots seemed to form.

Marvin was dying, and we both knew it. His shirts were all too big, and he kept putting new notches in his belt. I thought it would be nice if he could catch something this time

33

out, because the fact was he probably wouldn't be coming back again. I rowed as much as I could, giving him a chance to do more fishing, but the closest either of us got to a bite was on Marvin's line, a tug too strong to be a snag, and when he reeled in the plastic worm was gone.

Finally we just stopped there in the middle of the lake, the flies settling down around the oarlocks, a trail of broken crust, like red ice floes, behind us. There were no more leaks; the boat had sealed tight.

"Did I ever tell you about the time I visited the maze at Cornell University, back in Ithaca?" Marvin said, shifting a toothpick from the right side of his mouth to the left. "Unlike most mazes, in which a bunch of comic tourists generally find themselves wandering between walls or rows of hedges too high to see over, the one at Cornell was simplicity itself. It's since been outlawed, of course, but instead of walking around or moving in any fashion at all, the visitor was merely strapped down to a table and blindfolded. Then, under a light dose of anesthesia, an area of the brain was stimulated by an electrode to create a perfectly represented past event. Later, when the anesthesia wore off, the maze itself consisted of, under the guidance of trained technicians, the person trying to duplicate in his own memory what the electrodes had stimulated." Marvin had been my father's friend for years, and had gradually become mine as well, yet I was still surprised by the unusual and often arcane information he presented.

Marvin stared at his line, which was lying slack on the top of the hard surface of the lake. "The longest I ever spent in the maze was twenty-three days, fed by intravenous tubing and drained by catheters, while I tried to re-create one morning on my milk route in the city back in 1965."

I stopped to think. In 1965 I had just graduated from a small liberal arts college famous chiefly for the number of films that were shot using the campus as a location, and one of them, *Department Head*, had gone on to be a low-budget porn classic. In 1965 the Vietnam War was just beginning to gather momentum, and I, along with many others, attended a rally during which we waved our draft cards in the air and shouted, "Hell no, we won't go." Then we set them on fire.

My own card turned out to be more flammable than I had thought, and I had scarcely begun to burn it when I felt its heat threatening to blister the tips of my fingers. I hurled it away to where, unfortunately, it landed in a pile of unused banners and posters, setting them ablaze. Instead of confining itself to the corner, the fire quickly spread to an adjacent set of draperies, and suddenly the flames were everywhere. It turned out the place was a trap, and in the ensuing panic (all the exits had been blocked by symbolic re-creations of the Berlin Wall) over twenty fellow protesters were trampled to death.

In an effort to assign blame for all of this, I'm sorry to say the media had a field day, even going so far as to imply that I was a right-wing operative who had snuck into the rally to create exactly the catastrophe I've described. Others declared that the loss of so many "peaceniks," as they called them, was for the good of the country, and to my chagrin they suggested I should be commended. The end result was that, while being branded a felon, and so not allowed to serve in the Army, I was let off with several months of community service. I worked with the INHRI, the Institute for Napalm Handling Related Injuries—mostly sprains and eyes that needed flushing—which were increasing at an alarming rate as our troops, in an effort to burn more and more Vietnamese alive, were naturally required to handle more and more napalm.

Now motionless in the center of the lake, Marvin let out a sigh so low and full of pain it seemed almost to be from another person. "Let's go," he said, and without waiting for an answer began reeling his line in so rapidly the flecks of blood collecting in the eyelets of his rod spattered his face and his shirt. We rowed, and then, the surface of the lake having practically turned into a solid scab, we gave it up and poled our way back to shore, where we barely made an effort to hide the boat for the following year. The sun was setting by the time we had hiked out and begun our drive home. The radio was full of nothing but static, and Marvin was so tired he barely spoke, mostly just slumped beside me on the seat, half-dozing, his blood-smeared mouth opening wide every so often as he gasped for new supplies of air.

II

In the surprisingly unknown German expressionist film version of the classic play *Oedipus Rex*, director Hermann Stoltz begins with a scene in a rural tavern where Oedipus, busy at a game of miniature bowling, fails to notice that behind him patrons one after another are dropping off their stools and falling dead onto the floor, victims of an apparent plague. Behind him, one after the other, in a sequence lasting over twenty minutes, each actor, in his death throes, re-enacts the entire drama of his individual separate life, from birth onward, thus giving meaning and dignity to such a faceless punishment from the gods. In fact, it is only when Oedipus calls for a new package of Beer Nuts and hears no reply that he turns to the nearly empty tavern and notices something is amiss. And it is here that Stoltz's genius shows, as, deviating from the original plot, Oedipus expresses not the least bit of curiosity about what is happening and simply walks out, returning home to his palace and Jocasta, his wife. It was exactly this feeling of wrongness that I myself experienced when, after driving for several minutes lost in contemplation of the darkening night sky as it appeared interrupted by the smears of dead insects on my windshield, I turned to notice that Marvin had stopped breathing.

I slowed the Chevy Nova down and pulled off to the side of the road. Not far from where I was, I could see the shadows of a grove of pines, so I walked over to them and sat, my back against one of their massive trunks, listening to the rich sounds of the night. I breathed in the cooling air. Clearly, it seemed I would have to drive back to the city with Marvin slowly stiffening on the seat next to me, and by the time we arrived at his door it might be difficult to move him from the car. I would turn him over to Maureen, his wife, who would be upset, and then she would have to pay to bury him. On the other hand, I did have a small shovel I kept in the trunk for camping. If I dragged him out right there and dug a shallow grave and covered it, I'd be finished in less than an hour, depending on how shallow the grave was. I'd tell Maureen he'd drowned; she'd be upset, but would save a lot of money, and I wouldn't have to drive back with him slumping there next to me. I knew that's what Marvin would have wanted.

Everything went perfectly, and in well under an hour I was back on the road humming Chopin's *Funeral March* under my breath, keeping a sharp eye out for deer or other animals that might suddenly bolt from the bushes. I drove on through the country night, following the highway's twists and turns for what seemed like forever. Then it occurred to me: it *was* forever. I checked the clock on the dash. Even with the stop for burying Marvin, I should have been on the main highway an hour ago. I was lost.

I decided my best strategy was the one I remembered from an earlier discussion with Marvin about mazes: if I kept turning right, eventually I would come to the exit. I drove, turned right, drove and turned right, drove, turned right, and continued this for what seemed a long time. So long, in fact, I was just about to become discouraged when I spotted a light ahead of me, the light of a rural tavern.

I was thirsty, and by then more than a little hungry, so I gratefully turned the Nova onto its gravel driveway and walked in. The place was more or less traditional, with heads of small animals hanging on the walls, paintings of card-playing dogs over the bar, dark wood, and a rack that held the beer steins of the regulars. There was a fair-size crowd of customers that night, a mystery to me, as I couldn't imagine where they had come from out of the black emptiness I'd driven through to get there. I ordered a mug of beer and a liverwurst sandwich, and finished them both quickly. I was hungrier than I had thought, and I ordered another of the same. I would eat the second sandwich more slowly, I decided, maybe play a game or two in the mechanical bowling machine, get directions, and then leave. I put a quarter in the slot and began to slide the heavy metal puck down toward the pins, surprised at how soothing this simple action seemed. I played another game, and then another, and when I looked up again the tavern was nearly empty, save for my server, an attractive woman who had earlier introduced herself as Regina—a name I remembered because the only two Reginas I had ever known until then had both been mothers: the mother of the famous American writer Flannery O'Connor, and my own, who had disappeared when I was very young.

"Say," she said, watching me stifle a yawn as I prepared to leave, "it's late and it really is hard to find your way around here at night. Why don't you come home with me, and then you can leave in the morning?"

I studied her then for probably the first time that evening, from her low-cut red leather shoes which let one see the cracks where her toes joined her foot, to her satiny black dress with its plain white apron stained with the residue of ancient mustard and mayo spills, to the little paper crown that fitted into her blond hair by means of two wires, one of which had been replaced by a swizzle stick. She was slightly older than me, and she looked tired.

Regina's trailer was not far from the tavern, and decorated with an odd assortment of prints and photos representing every style from the cool eye of the Dutch Renaissance to the happy machinery of the Russian futurists, with kitsch and dada in between. There was a postcard of a little girl crossing the street on her tricycle as an angel held back a large van on its way to delivering electrical appliances to a laboratory, and another of two men fishing from an island which, unbeknownst to them, was actually the back of a giant fish. She herself had begun to paint, Regina said, although she didn't know if she would call it art or not. She had begun taking a few classes at the local college after her husband, who had been a pilot in Vietnam, was declared missing in action when his plane developed engine trouble following a successful mission in which he had leveled an enemy hospital. "I wish I could have seen the looks on their faces," Regina said, "thinking they were safe at last, when what should come from out of the sky but Jeff and all those bombs."

III

Wily Odysseus, his friends kept calling him back in those Trojan War days, but now, I think, he's known not so much for his cleverness as for his having spent twenty years being lost on what we since have named in his honor "an odyssey." But suppose he'd never gone. Suppose when the recruiters came to get him he'd kept on ploughing straight over his son who the recruiters had put in his way, kept on sowing the fields with salt, kept on wearing an eggshell for a hat, would the Greeks have won? He could have had other kids, sown other fields, put some ointment on his sunburned head, but would anybody remember the Trojan War, or even the *Iliad*, let alone the *Odyssey*?

The following morning, as I drove away from Regina's art-filled trailer, I found myself thinking about all those who had died in the draft card fire. Would having fought have made up for it? And what about the person who must have been called up to serve in my place? Had he lived? Died? How many more enemy did he kill than I would have, and if he killed no one, then how many did his presence allow others to murder?

Back in my apartment everything was as I'd left it. A shaft of sun streamed through the window in the kitchen, turning the bread crumbs I'd forgotten to sweep up into specks of gold. A few unwashed plates (among which I recognized the remains of a tasty "Beef Burgundy") were in the sink, and on the counter was a cookbook specializing in fish that I, in my optimism, had apparently been looking through before I left.

I called Maureen, Marvin's wife, who had been worried when we hadn't returned late last night, as we'd promised. I told her what had happened, and then after a long silence she thanked me. "I'll be in touch later," she said, "but right now I have to get adjusted."

And then a most peculiar thing happened. It may have been because of my stress over the death of my friend, or simply from the fatigue due to the fact that the previous night Regina had made me sit through two complete showings of a video that documented Bob Hope entertaining the troops in Vietnam, its *raison d'être* being a living close-up of Jeff, happily unaware of his fate as he waved his arms and made suggestive motions with his tongue toward one of the leggy female dancers Hope had brought with him on his tour, but whatever the case, after I had replaced the phone on its cradle following my conversation with Maureen and walked into my bedroom, I saw there before me, sitting on my bed, a man wearing army fatigues, smoking a cigarette, making a cup out of one of his hands to catch the ashes. He appeared to have been wounded in several places, though no blood was seeping at that moment. Part of his face and jaw had been blown away, so that his teeth, which were intact, and part of the actual jawbone were exposed .

"Hi," he said, "my name is Gary and I'm the one who took your place in Vietnam."

"Oh," I said. "So I guess this means you were killed."

"Yeah," he said, and looked at me. He was about twenty, and on the side of his face that was still left I could see a couple of reddish marks that looked like pimples. "Yeah," he said again.

I thought, the more I got used to him, that Gary was kind

of a goofy looking kid. "Do you want an ashtray or anything?" I said.

"Hey," he said, "I died so you could be free."

"Gary," I said, "I'm sorry that you died, but it wasn't to make me free. Let's get that straight."

"OK," he said. "It was the first thing that came to mind. I guess I didn't really mean it." He kept on smoking, and the hand that was holding the cigarette was shaking a bit.

I pushed an empty glass toward him. "Here, you can use this." The bottom of the glass already had some old stuff dried on it, so it wasn't any great loss. Also, I noticed, the laces of Gary's boots were unlaced, and the soles still had some mud on them. I looked around. Little chunks of it were lying here and there. My gaze went back to him. He seemed nervous, and was bouncing just a bit on the mattress. "Gary," I said, "what do you want from me?"

He settled back and stopped bouncing for a minute, then he blew some smoke out the missing side of his face. "Let me tell you a story," he said.

"It was the summer before I was to be drafted into the army," he said, "the summer of 1965. During that time, I didn't know what to do—I couldn't get a real job, but part-time jobs were to be found where I was living, so I did what I could, I got a temporary job in a slaughterhouse. It wasn't killing animals or anything like that—that was all specialized work and those jobs were hard to get—all I did was spread sawdust wherever I saw a pool of blood on the floor, waited a couple minutes, then swept it up so no one would slip and hurt himself.

"Needless to say, blood was pretty much everywhere. I had worked there a couple of weeks, and to my surprise I found I wasn't getting used to it, in fact the job was getting harder rather than easier. The thought of waking up each day to the endless screams of frightened animals, to the smells of shit and blood, the sound of butcher saws, was beginning to upset me. I was ready to do almost anything to quit, and yet,

I rationalized, I needed the money." Here he shook his head, as if amazed at the naivete of his own youth.

"Finally it got to be too much. It was on a Wednesday, and I promised myself I'd finish out the week, then quit. This slaughterhouse specialized mostly in cows—I'm not sure why—but every so often we'd get a run of hogs or sheep, and then we'd go back to cows. So this Wednesday I had just finished spreading out a pile of sawdust, and was waiting for it to soak up the blood, when this group of sheep came through.

"I was sort of there and not there, you know, watching but only paying half-attention because really, I didn't want to see them die, but if you're there, you're going to watch, you can't help it." I nodded, and Gary seemed happy that I'd understood this concept.

"So I was watching only just a bit, and mostly I was thinking what I'd do about my paycheck, and if maybe I could get the Army to take me right away so I wouldn't have to get another job, when all of a sudden one sheep in particular caught my eye." He shrugged. "I can't explain why that should happen, but it did, and this one had a kind of aura maybe, and there he was, looking back at me, not even at the guy who's going to kill him, but me. And all the while he's getting closer to the guy who's using the mallet to snap the necks of those in front of him he's still looking me straight in the eye, not even blinking, and finally, when he's about a foot away from where he's going to die, he stares at me and just says, 'Gary.'"

Gary gave a little laugh and looked at me, as if to check if I believed him. "So I turned to the guy who was killing the sheep and said, 'Did you hear that?' And he says, 'Hear what?' And I said, 'Did that sheep say "Gary" or anything like it?'

"And he said no, but that sometimes they make all kinds of sounds when they are being killed, but you can't take them seriously, because once he'd heard one say 'Minneapolis' as clear as a bell and he'd never been there in his life. But I asked myself what were the odds of that sheep just happening to say

42

'Gary' when I was standing right there, and that's exactly when I knew that I was going to die."

I looked at him. His colors seemed to be changing, like a TV set that needs adjusting. "Huh?" I said.

"So it's OK," he answered, and then he disappeared.

IV

I had arrived home from my fishing trip mid-morning, but somehow by the time Gary vanished into a test pattern it had turned to evening, a phenomenon I attributed to the fact that in order to convince myself that the feeble transmission of the spirit world was real, I had to slow down time, so that one signal building on top of another could create the illusion of three dimensions. When I went back to real time, Gary disappeared.

Outside, the moon was nearly full, and I thought of the description of that heavenly body given by Richard Grossinger, in his marvelous book *The Night Sky*, as being associated "with memory, the unconscious, and the duplication of codes." And what code, I asked myself, had I uncracked that evening? What had I remembered? Most of the time I could only answer, "nothing," and that mostly my life seemed only a bloody trail through time, killing, eating, using, stumbling, leaving, burying everything that crossed the wake of my unhappy presence. "The moon," Grossinger went on, "stands for enslavement of man's will in blind, meaningless, destructive activity, mechanicalness, and habit." In short, the exact sort of moon that rose over Blood Lake the first time Marvin took me there, over twenty years ago.

It is a memory that I can recall as perfectly as if it were just stimulated by an electrode applied to the surface of my brain. There the two of us stood, at the top of the tortuous path that climbed the mountains to the lake. The path was narrow then, and easy to mistake, so I remember we spent much of our time spraying blue arrows of paint and slashing the trunks of the pines with our machetes. Marvin was older than me, of course, and skilled in the ways of nature. Even so it was almost dark when, from the top of a nearby mountain peak, we caught sight of our destination, and I was just about to scramble down a slope of loosened rocks to the shore of the lake itself when I felt a grip of steel around my arm to indicate that I should stop.

"Wait," said Marvin. "It's important that you should hear this story before we go any further."

I found a nearby rock and made myself comfortable, and then, letting my backpack slide from my shoulders onto a small patch of moss the shape of Greece, I answered, "OK, I'm listening."

Marvin sighed and stared a while deep into the shadows of the darkening night, as if he were looking for a text he might read. "I used to have a milk route," he began, "one in which I went from door to door in early mornings and delivered to my customers fresh milk, butter, cottage cheese, and any other dairy products they might find themselves in need of. This was before the days of knowing about cholesterol, naturally, and little did I realize that in this way I was participating in the slow poisoning of whole generations of average American families."

He paused, considering what he had said before he went on again. "It was on that route I met your parents, who were my customers, and it was on a cold November morning when, in addition to a nicely written request for a quart of milk and a dozen eggs, they added at the bottom of the page, 'P.S. Would you come inside a minute?'" He paused again, and in that space a night bird inserted its lonely cry.

"The light around your parents' kitchen table was a yolky yellow that morning, and I remember how you, a helpless newborn infant, lay quietly in its center, wheezing from time to time, next to a golden pile of crumbs from a stack of half-eaten toast. A week before you were born, the earnest couple told me, they had gone to a fortune teller at the county fair, and he had predicted that you would eventually grow up to disgrace the two of them, a modest couple who made their living writing book reviews. They wished you no harm, they said, but in order to avoid spending all those years treating you well and loving you, only to be disappointed, they asked me if I could possibly give you away to some childless couple on my milk route.

"I thought about it. Even a week earlier my answer would have been no, but as fate would have it, just the day before, along with a request for a carton of sour cream and a pound of butter, a couple a mile or so away had left a long note, complaining bitterly about their childless state. I took your parents up on their request, and eight stops later you were sound asleep inside the milk bin of the couple in question." Marvin gave a loud snuffle, and then continued.

"A few years later, your real parents moved away, to New York City, I think. I never saw them again, although I kept in touch with your adopted guardians, at first from afar, but later, when your adopted mother left in order to become a classical scholar, I became close friends with the man you know as your father, who even then was still writing long complaining letters about whatever trifle happened to cross his mind.

"Well, now you know," he said. "It's time to walk down to the lake."

And now Gary was gone, Marvin was gone, my adopted mother was in some library researching ancient texts, my adopted father had moved to a condo with a hot tub at the edge of a golf course in Arizona, and my real parents were very possibly bylines in the *New York Times Book Review*. Overhead the blank face of the moon stared down at me, the same moon that had been the witness to all of these events and yet had remained unchanged by the greatest of them. Only when men themselves had landed on its surface, had gouged out a few pounds of rock, scuffed a pile of pebbles, scorched some sand, could it be said that an alteration had taken place, and since that time it had returned again to silence.

Could one be *only* a witness, I wondered, or did the mere presence of an onlooker somehow change the event itself? Was there ever a story that could be retold without its changing? Or without its changing in some small way the one to whom it's told? The glass by my bedside still held Gary's ashes even though both he and his cigarette had disappeared. The hands of my Baby Ben alarm clock registered four a.m., and behind the forking branches of the trees outside my window, a red glow was beginning to seep upward into the flat fabric of the night. Somewhere to the east, above the lake, another day was starting.

A COWBOY'S STORY

I

Howdy. The moon was full and the sky looked like that famous sieve for detecting prime numbers invented by the ancient Greek geographer, Eratosthenes, who was, among other things, the first to measure the size of the earth. Prime numbers, I thought. How like them we humans are: erratic, indivisible, unpredictable, and infinite. And yet, at the same time limited, discoverable, and essentially just another concept not good for much of anything beyond cryptography.

Meanwhile all around me prairie dogs were tearing in and out of their holes, and I could hear the plaintive howl of coyotes, the dry slither of sidewinders, and the downy rush of the great horned owl as it passed nearby, possibly mistaking my head as it poked from my sleeping bag for a grizzled and terribly deformed jackrabbit—an easy meal on a night such as this. I unzipped the bag and walked over to where my fellow cowboys were lying peacefully asleep, their mouths half-open, their lips half-smacking, their bodies half-twitching in some dream of calf roping or bull riding; they seemed content. The horses, too, tethered near the little stand of cottonwoods— they also appeared content. I pivoted slowly on the heel of one boot. All around me the world was busy snoring, dreaming, flying, crawling, running, killing, hiding, bleeding, calling, and/or dying, and in every case, its participants seemed perfectly content. What was wrong with me, I wondered. And then all at once that very night seemed as good a time as any to go off somewhere and end my purposeless, pointless life.

Having made up my mind, the rest was easy. Whoever said, "Plan ahead," was right, because it was on an evening long ago, while rocking in the saddle of my faithful horse in the midst of a cattle drive (which, far from being the romantic image perpetrated by books and motion pictures, is instead only a hot, dusty, highly unpleasant exercise in which a group of formerly happy creatures [cows] are driven against their will to slaughter even as their calves call plaintively for them, while they, the moms, mistakenly reassure their children that the separation is only temporary), that I had formulated my plan for exiting this world. First, I decided, I would leave a note, the contents of which would advise those left behind not to waste their valuable time looking for me. I would post this in a conspicuous place, and then, leaving my saddle and the rest of my possessions behind, I would walk up into the mountains, find a cave, crawl inside, and seal off the entrance. At last, alone in the dark, I'd remove one of my boots and find the single-edged razor blade I kept beneath my insoles (an old cowboy trick) and then... You can guess the rest.

I checked my watch; it was nearly three a.m. I tiptoed over to my saddlebag and extracted the pad of paste-on notes I liked to keep there and the lucky ballpoint pen I'd taken several years ago from the Bowl-Rite Lanes, in Abilene.

Dear Friends, (I wrote)

I'm going to where the grass is always green and the streams always run clear. Don't go looking for me. I leave my saddle to Bob, my sleeping bag to Waco, my extra boots to Carlos, my toiletry kit to Jesse, my collection of early Bill Evans records to

Slim, and any back wages I may have coming to
the Audubon Society.

Adios,
Jim

Then I pinned this note to Clement where he stood tied
to a cottonwood tree, and rubbed his neck good-bye.
Touching the brim of my Stetson, I bid a silent farewell to the
sleeping camp and headed east, toward the mountains. The
walk across the desert, perhaps in that heightened state when
one thinks it is to be one's last walk anywhere, was nothing
short of extraordinary. The way ahead of me was lit by a
lunar glow which gave each cactus, each clump of sage, each
scorpion and each endangered desert tortoise the look of having been, for some reason, first dipped in milk, then rolled
lightly in flour in preparation to being sautéed in sizzling
peanut oil. By the time the gas grill of the day's heat had
turned on, however, I'd reached the foothills, and as I climbed
the air grew cooler. Low scrub gave way to deciduous trees,
and deciduous trees to pine forests. Then evening arrived, and
it was time to look for a cave, or possibly an abandoned mine,
where I could shut my personal door on the world once and
for all. Fortunately, this mountain I was ascending had been
the site of a mining boom in years past, and its surface was
riddled with forgotten claims and halfhearted tunnels.

The excavation I chose was of medium size, not so high
that one could stand erect, but neither did I have to resort to
crawling, like a baby, on all fours. It was dry and deep, and
had a pleasant musty smell of earth, but with a tinge of smoke
around its edges. From its entrance I looked out at the world
one last time. The pines were fuzzy in the dying light, and far
beneath me I could see the desert floor, a brown-blue blur of
sage and scrub, with dots of light on the horizon that I guessed
were the cooking fires of my former companions. Night birds
had begun to call, and another cycle of night and day was

coming to a close. I lay my hand on one of the loose rocks near the ceiling. As many times as I had planned this moment, still I found it unbelievably difficult to imagine never seeing the world again. That single act, simply to loosen one average-size stone, the one that would cause my world to shrink to permanent darkness, was harder than anything I had ever done.

I gave a halfhearted tug and the rock plopped to the ground at my feet, but the ceiling stayed intact. I pulled out another, then another—nothing. Then all at once there was a great noise and things went dark and the air was full of dust and hard to breath, and after that came the loudest silence I have ever heard in my entire life. For some reason (privacy, I suppose) I decided to crawl away from the entrance of the cave to a deeper place where I would rest my back against a wall one last time, take off my left boot, which by then was pinching uncomfortably, remove the odor-absorbing insole, take out the razor and prepare for the moment its icy edge would wander down the lonely and treeless path of my stringy veins. Making my way several yards back from the entrance, I leaned against a wall and removed the boot. It felt good to have it off, and I wiggled my toes a moment before I felt inside for the razor. The thought struck me—a ridiculous one, but that's how the mind works at such moments: it would be silly for me to die with only one boot on. And so, using the toes of my left foot, I loosened the right one and kicked it off into the darkness where I heard first a soft thud, and then a groan.

Her name was Marjorie, and she later told me she had taken shelter in the tunnel the previous night after having become separated from the other members of her archeological team during a heavy fog. Then, she said, after proceeding forward in a hunched-over fashion for a few yards, she found herself stricken by her own personal disability, catatonia, the very disease suffered by Silas Marner in the loathsome novel of the same name. It had been my intemperate criticism of this book which had got me tossed out of my seventh-grade English class, beginning the long, sad slide of scholastic failure that led to my becoming a junior high school dropout, a high school dropout by default, the disgrace of my family, and eventually, a cowboy.

Marjorie's first words were, "Is it night?" and it was my unhappy duty to inform her not only that it was, but also that I had sealed up the entrance to the cave. When daylight finally came, I told her, neither she nor I would ever know it. She sank into a long, and what felt like a judgmental silence (so long, in fact, I struck a match to discover if she were some kind of phantom seen only by those about to die; she wasn't). Studying her as she lay there in the weak, flickering light, her shirt having become unbuttoned by tossing and turning during her recent nap, noting her attractively torn jeans, the abrasions on her elbows, the smudges of dirt along her high and well-formed cheekbones, and her hair tied in a loose ponytail with a stylish paisley ribbon, I gasped. At least by the light of this one match, she was beautiful. Then, as those thousands who took shelter in the London Underground during the grim days of World War Two, when the Nazi war birds of prey ruled the skies of Europe, strangers huddled together awaiting the first distant muffled thuds that would indicate an attack was under way; like those desperate, frightened men and women, perhaps holding hands at first, then fondling, then petting, then, unable to help themselves going further and further to discover the ecstasy of each other's flesh, Marjorie and I made love. And then, as ridiculous as it may seem, as predictable and boring as it undoubtedly is, the famous vivifying qualities of that ancient act made themselves felt as last: I wanted to live.

Fortunately, there was another way out of the mine. It so happened that the entrance into which I had crawled was only one part of an L-shaped tunnel, and there was another opening which Marjorie eventually remembered. Not, however, before, believing she was about to die, she began to relate her life's story, which, I'm sorry to say, her catatonia aside, was of such stupefying normalcy I nodded off after the first five minutes.

Close by the fabulous faux Tudor home where I live these days, there is a notorious pedagogue of literature who is known for his dictum, "Tell a dream; lose a reader," and it certainly is true that I myself can attest to a definite glassiness that overcomes me when, say I'm at a banquet or a dinner party and someone sitting next to me will smugly turn and say, "I just have to tell you about the most amazing dream." Nonetheless, some time shortly after Marjorie's description of a day in the eleventh grade when she had not completed her homework and the teacher became angry, I myself had the following dream: It was night and I was riding Clement. As usual, I could hear the muffled cough of prairie dogs and the jubilant screech of owls, but that night something was different. I was leading Clement toward a destination which, although I had no idea what it was, seemed tremendously important. The only clue I had was a sheet of paper with the words, "Hollywood, California," written in light-blue pencil, yet I was going east, toward the Atlantic, when Hollywood was west.

I awoke to phrases like "post-internecine," and "pre-mid-plasticine," as Marjorie described just a few of the highlights of the archeological expedition from which she was currently missing, an excavation of sacred Indian burial sites not far away. She finished her narrative and pointed to the luminous dial of her watch. "It's day," she said, and suggested we walk on out and greet it.

The sensation I experienced on stepping back into sunlight reminded me of nothing so much as walking out of a darkened movie theater into a dazzling afternoon post-matinee sun, into streets still hot and bright, and a time that had somehow been going on without me at a different rate than deep inside the theater.

We walked down the mountain in near silence, each of us assessing what had happened between us the night before, and this double reticence continued as we stood at the base near the highway which would, by mutual agreement, take her back to her grave-robbing friends. I also had a sudden urge to see my own friends, my fellow cowpunchers, but quickly realized that the nature of the note I had left them, together with the instructions what to do, would make my reappearance an embarrassment. A Buick station wagon passed us by, and then a Nova driven by a tired-looking man in a fishing hat. Then all at once I was standing in the dust of a blue Ford pickup, waving at Marjorie as she returned my gesture through the pickup's rear window. Whatever happencd, I told myself, I would have to make a new life, a new start, a new resolution, and it would be alone.

II

A wise man once remarked that life is like a bird that flies in one window of a cathedral and then out another, but for me, who has seen birds caught in supermarkets and churches, fluttering hopelessly for days before smashing or starving to death, this wisdom is not reassuring. Once in, it's not so easy to get out. Another wise man remarked that we have to approach life as if we were approaching the edge of a cliff, or possibly a swimming pool, and the only thing to do is jump, although if it is a swimming pool, I don't see why people can't lower themselves slowly, to acclimate to the change in temperature, enjoy the tang of chlorine, and assess the struggling splashes of the other swimmers before plunging in.

The pool I'm speaking of here belonged to my new employers, Bud and Cissie Light, or Bud and Cissie, as they liked to be called, and the occasion for these musings was a day off from my job as a butler, in which capacity I'd been hired after answering an ad in the *Tucson News* shortly after I walked into town from the desert. Because I had left behind most of my possessions, the idea of a place to stay and plenty of free uniforms appealed to me. For their part Bud and Cissie were delighted to have an authentic ex-cowboy on their payroll, and often drew me away from my chores to demonstrate lassoing a fence post or rolling a cigarette.

Bud was the publisher of *Take Five*, a magazine that devoted itself to the world of jazz, and he financed the whole enterprise through a small fortune his parents, the owners of a huge cosmetics company, had left him. It was pleasant working in an atmosphere where a range of jazz, from traditional to the most progressive, was constantly piped through speakers.

Cissie was an art form in herself. Originally trained as a classical pianist, her promising career had been cut short when, in the middle of a successful transcription of the *Grand Canyon Suite* she got stuck on the two notes that were supposed to duplicate the hoof beats of the tiny burros used to take tourists down inside the canyon itself. "I kept seeing those poor little animals carrying those big tourists going round and round," she told me one afternoon, "and I couldn't get them to go down into the canyon so the people could get off and the burros could rest, but neither could I let them stop." One by one, she said, the members of the audience, sensing that this was no mere performance trick, got up and left, until in the end it took two burly stagehands, one to hold Cissie back as the other pushed the Steinway out of her reach, to bring the concert to an end.

In order to recover from this trauma Cissie had worked as a topless dancer in a sandwich shop, gyrating listlessly to the sounds of Top Forty hits and heavy metal, when one day Bud had stopped in and taught her the freedom inherent in improvisation. Now most days she would walk around the house humming happily or even going off on her own in brilliant solos to the piped-in music, except for those moments when she would stand stock still for hours, a victim of catatonia. It was a rare disease, she explained, and the only other person she knew of with such an affliction was her sister, a scientist of some sort whom she hadn't seen since the end of her music career.

My duties around the house were not stressful. Each evening I would pile up briquettes into a little pyramid and start a fire in the barbecue. In the mornings I would make a pot of coffee and set out the box of Sugar Frosted Flakes, Bud's favorite cereal. Cissie usually ate only a piece of whole wheat toast with apple butter, and a cup of coffee. After they finished eating I did the dishes and had my own breakfast: fresh fruit, yogurt, and a muffin. Then I would begin my job of screening the backlog of letters to *Take Five* that Bud had been unable to find the time to open.

Most were straightforward enough: either protesting an article that had been published or proposing an article of their own. The most promising of these I passed on to Bud. In between were the usual threats, promises of support and the rare subscription form (and I must say it was a constant surprise how a publication so few people read could generate such a volume of correspondence). Rarest of all were those letters that actually appeared to be an answer to a specific question or a previous request from Bud himself. So you can imagine my amazement when, early one afternoon, I opened the following letter that had arrived about a month before I did.

Dear Bud, (it said)

Thanks for asking me to share these few thoughts and recollections about my life in music. Despite the fact that there are many in this world who would scorn to answer such a request as yours, I still like to think I have a debt to pay to a man who has chosen me a three-time runner-up for the

Take Five Golden Music Stand award, given annually for excellence in creativity, technique, and philosophical innovation.

So let me start by admitting that I was not especially talented growing up. True, I heard the usual big hits of the forties and fifties, but no one in my family, from my parents to my hopeless brother, ever encouraged any interest in anything besides the world of books. I myself continued this trend when I became an English major at a college whose chief claim to fame was that it had been the location for several low-budget thrillers and porn flicks, most notably the cult classic, *Oral Exams*. (I actually appear in one of the crowd scenes.)

No, Bud, it was only after graduation that I can say my career began. I was invited to a party to benefit a fellow student who, in the process of burning his draft card, had inadvertently set himself on fire. The party was at a local barbecue house, and the area near the cooking pit was filled that evening with a host of gorgeous women talking about such things as astronomy and Michaelangelo and auto repair. I stood there, holding a wedge of sweet potato pie, and tried to figure out a way to insert myself into the conversation.

Suddenly a beautiful woman with black hair and a beaded headband turned to ask, "What actually is the affect on an engine if it's driven at too low a rate of speed?"

I shrugged and gave a little chuckle, as if to indicate we were in on a kind of private joke.

"It beats me," I said, and hastily lowered my pie. "Would you like to leave this party and go where just the two of us can talk?"

"Huh?" she said. "Why should I go anywhere with a guy like you?"

"You'll never find out unless you try," I rejoindered, although to tell the truth it did seem like a good question, one which I have never been able to answer without the use of cheap sophistry.

We wound up back at an apartment she was
renting at a reduced rate because it was next door
to the laboratory where she worked putting drops
of shampoo into the eyes of rabbits. "They actually enjoy it," she explained, "because after each
time we put shampoo in their eyes we reward
them with a bit of food. We can use a rabbit for
two or three months, maybe twenty times a day,"
she added, "before its eyes become so irritated
they're like open sores and of no use. When that
happens we kill them and sell them to various
restaurants, after first removing all four paws,
which we sell to a lucky rabbit's foot key chain
company in Atlanta. We sell the skins to a company that makes children's gloves," she said,
"after we've removed the ears. And by the way if
you can think of a good use for them you can
make a lot of money, because we have a ton of
them in storage."

Her name was Monica, and her apartment was
not large, but dark and had that special sweet
smell of a place where a woman has lived alone.
We lay down on the bed and began to kiss quietly,
the only sounds coming from the occasional jet
plane passing overhead (she lived in the flight path
of a major airport) and the desperate thumps of
furry bodies against wire cages from the lab,
which shared a wall with her bedroom.

Morning came, and Monica went to work
while I stayed behind to do the dishes, fix a pesky
drip, oil the hinges on her cabinets and repaint her
apartment. "Wow, the place looks different," she
said when she walked back in that evening, her
clothes smelling of wheat germ and honey. Then
we kissed and went to sleep. A month passed more
or less that way, then two. Winter came and I
weatherstripped her windows and planted bulbs
by the front door.

"It's amazing I found you," I'd say.

"No," she'd answer. "It's amazing I found
you."

Then we'd giggle and we'd kiss. "And just think," she said, "in a couple more months you'll be ready to start fondling my breasts."

A week went by, a month, and then another. I decided I could wait no longer. One day, just as we were finishing up a session of kissing, I began to fondle. "Well," she said, "this *is* a surprise!"

I wasted no time. From then on, each day as Monica would leave for the lab I would begin work on the apartment. I flocked the wallpaper, tore down a wall, installed a wrought-iron circular staircase, and built a breakfast nook. During the pauses in my sawing I would listen next door for the thumps of bunnies in their cages or the sharp squeals that followed a particularly strong batch of shampoo being squirted into their eyes, and I'd think of Monica.

Then one day I found it necessary to take a trip out of town. I hated the thought of being separated from Monica, but there was a new squeakless kind of hardware for kitchen cabinets I wanted to check out, and the trip would mean missing only one night at home. I set out late in the afternoon by bus and arrived at an inexpensive hotel in the city where the manufacturer of the hardware had his plant. The following day I planned to take a cab out to be shown the hinges, and then return to the bus station by three. I'd be home for dinner, I thought happily to myself.

I had eaten the sandwiches Monica had made earlier—some sort of meat, and lettuce—and was sitting on the bed in my hotel room, waiting for the radio to conclude a medley of Beatles hits before I fell asleep, when I heard a knock at the door. I opened it, and a young woman wearing a trenchcoat burst in. She shut the door behind her.

"You must let me spend the night," she said. "If you don't, they'll kill me."

I agreed, and to my surprise, when she removed her coat she was wearing only a flimsy, somewhat yellowed nightgown beneath it. I turned down

"Eleanor Rigby" and crawled under the sheets, and she joined me. As in those dangerous days of the London Blitz, when complete strangers were forced together by danger, we kissed, then fondled, and more. After a couple of hours she told me the danger had passed, asked for some money to buy drugs, and left.

The next morning I found myself in an unusual mood. My previous interest in kitchen hardware seemed to have vanished. Cashing in the unused portion of my bus ticket, I took a job at a small record store that specialized in jazz. I quickly learned to play the tenor saxophone and eventually joined a small combo which played at clubs, the occasional private party, and even had a moderate success with a recording of a song I penned, "Moody Mr. D.," on which I had a short solo, and from which I received my nickname. I began to drink, learned to smoke marijuana, and wore mostly black shirts and black trousers which I would buy at the Asthmatic Thrift Store, about a block from my apartment. I continued lessons on the saxophone, obtaining a modest stipend to attend the state university on the other side of town. I never saw Monica again.

One night years later, we were playing in a small club attached to the local Holiday Inn, and were halfway through a long ballad, "The Return of the Ancient Mariner," in which the trumpet player had an extended solo he claimed had been modeled on the cry of an albatross he'd heard once on a TV nature special, when I spotted a tiny, disheveled woman at one of the tables near the salad bar. It was Carla, one of Monica's best friends, and I took the opportunity of a break to speak with her and her date, a salesman for a company that provided animals to laboratories. His name was Richard, and he explained to me that the former animals of choice—dogs and cats and rabbits—were now falling out of favor because, as he put it, "they're just too much like us." To fill

59

the gap his company had concentrated on providing the uglier members of the animal kingdom—hyenas, bats and baboons—to labs all over the world, and had gone so far as to genetically engineer a new breed of rat that was so repulsive that people would practically beg to torture it. These rats, he said, were beginning to attract a large number of customers in "the home market," as he called it, who had no connection to labs or corporations, and this was developing into a surprisingly profitable sideline.

Carla told me that Monica had left her job, gotten married, and had three lovely children. Her husband had invented a computer program that was able to predict the appearance of certain diseases so accurately that insurance companies were able to cancel claims before the insured even knew he was sick. Monica seldom spoke of me, Carla said, but when she did it was invariably with loathing. Carla sipped her drink, a kiwi sour. She said that although she was sure I had my reasons for doing what I did, and personally she held no grudges, she wasn't at all surprised by Monica's strong feelings. I got up, took my sax, and played three choruses of "Goin' Shopping" to the amazed patrons of the club.

And now, as I write this, Bud, I can well imagine you and the faithful readers of *Take Five* asking what this has to do with music. Let me try to explain: This morning I looked inside my ears and saw what appeared to be a brownish crust of dirt. Finding a washcloth and wetting it slightly I rubbed to discover that both my ears had accumulated a surprising amount of the stuff, a combination, I guess, of dried soap and dead skin and ancient long-expelled earwax. It's funny, I thought, when I was a child I used to hate it when my mother would bend down to wash my ears, and I imagined that when I was grown that would be one thing I wouldn't have to do. But there I was, checking my ears. In other words, like it or not, we live with our decisions, good and bad, and who's to say which is which?

I lost Monica, and still I can't forget it. In return I received a fabulous career in music. But the other day, as I was somewhere attending a party to celebrate our group's newest album, *Intimations of Immorality*, amid the glamour and the laughter and the wine, the beautiful girls, and some of them mine, I caught sight of an ordinary hinge on a cabinet behind the bar. It was only a brass interlocking cylinder with a pin down the middle and a flange on either side, but who's to say I didn't have the right to notice?

Sincerely,
Moody Mr. D.

I thought back to my own bookish brother I had lost touch with so many years ago, my last glimpse of whom had been second hand— one of the crowd scenes in that cult classic, *Oral Exams*. I checked the postmark of the letter I was holding with trembling hands, and to my amazement it was Tucson, the very town I was living in.

III

Putting one of his flabby arms around my shoulders, Bud explained to me that my brother had died, together with an unknown passenger, in a tragic accident only days after the letter must have arrived, a sort of "testament from the grave," to use Bud's phrasing. Apparently my brother had swerved to avoid a stray cow on the highway, and his vehicle, a classic blue Ford pickup, ran into a large stone marker put along the highway to commemorate the very first historical marker in the state. He was killed instantly.

I felt awful, but on second thought, how did I *really* feel?

I hadn't seen Dave in twenty years. If I was in mourning, what then was the object of my grief? It certainly wasn't my memories, which, accurate or not, I carried intact. So it must have been the loss of the possibility of seeing him again, a possibility I'd never even thought of till that moment, but which meant that out of the infinite number of possible futures previously available, now there were fewer. "I'll need some time to be alone," I said, so Bud graciously pointed me toward my room and shut the door.

The room I had been given to stay in had blue and yellow wallpaper full of baby ducks and chicks and geese, and had belonged to Cissie and Bud's child before he died, I was told, in a swimming pool accident. The boy had fallen in one afternoon, and his calls for help might have been heard had not Bud been wearing his headphones at the time and been listening, he said, to Mr. D. himself. Cissie unfortunately had been possessed at that very moment by one of those catatonic trances and so while she had heard his tiny screams, she had been unable to help. "I had just removed the headphones," Bud said, "when I became aware of an unnatural silence in the house, so after calling out, each time my voice rising higher in panic, I rushed outdoors to find my son's small form, still clothed in his Rambo Junior camouflage outfit, still clutching his toy semiautomatic rifle in one hand and his toy survival knife in the other, lying in a clump of sodden leaves at the bottom of our quiet blue pool."

The boy's furniture, his armored vehicle bed, his aircraft carrier desk, his stealth aircraft light fixture, had, of course, all been removed from the room. Only the wallpaper had been left, and as I stared into the bright blue eyes and yellow beaks, repeated in seemingly endless combinations around the room, I couldn't help but reflect about the disparity between all our youths and all our futures.

I woke with a start. The afternoon's harsh light driving its way through the sliding glass door and the curtains reminded me of the time when, afraid of being recognized as someone whose chief concern was sex and mindless titillation, I attended a matinee showing of *Oral Exams*, and later stepped out into the afternoon sun, simultaneously blinking my eyes and searching the streets in order to spot anyone I might know before they spotted me. Fortunately the street on that day happened to be deserted due to a hostage situation in a bank a block away.

Bud and Cissie's large, rambling, ranch-style house was strangely quiet when I emerged from my room. The earth-tone furniture stood in the sunlight like confused children on a grade-school outing to a milk-processing plant. "What are we doing here?" the objects seemed to be asking. Dust motes roamed in silence, without even the usual buzz of background static coming in over the piped-in music system.

"Hello," I called, but there was no answer. I walked through room after room, until at last in her bedroom I found Cissie frozen in one of her trances, completely naked except for her bra, which she had either been hooking or unhooking when the trance hit. Her eyes were the kind of blue you sometimes see out the windows of jet planes, and as peaceful as twin headstones. Bud had gone somewhere, perhaps on some publishing matter, and had left a note on the dresser saying he would return in several hours.

I walked to the kitchen where I threw into a cast-iron skillet a little olive oil and a couple of sliced potatoes. While the potatoes were cooking I chopped up some red pepper, half an onion, a small zucchini, a couple artichoke hearts, some mushrooms, and several ripe olives, adding them one at a time to the potatoes, along with a touch of garlic, salt and pepper. When they were all cooked I mixed in three eggs, beaten with two tablespoons of cream, and covered the pan, letting the mixture cook at low heat until the eggs were no longer runny. I ate some and left the oven on low to keep the rest till Bud's return, and even now, years later, I cannot taste this delightful and easy-to-prepare fritatta without remembering what must have been the trauma of that afternoon.

And certainly, it's easy to tell myself that had I not decided to pack my bags and leave the minute I finished eating, washing and putting away the dishes in order to board a Greyhound bus for Hollywood, California, where I had hopes, due in part to having read the book, *Bergman: Genius or Madman?* (a critical study based on interviews with over a hundred former mental patients), by Sven Björnström, perhaps Cissie would not have been burned to death in the terrible fire which quickly swept through the cheaply built, poorly insulated home, although one might as well blame Bud for not arriving, or the builder, or the anonymous person who assembled the oven with a leaky gas jet. "The finger of blame," a wise man once said, "never lacks a direction to point in."

My first feature film, called *Snail*, produced for the Disney people, had as its subject a sort of retriever-looking dog who had been named for a peculiar snail-shaped marking on his side. The movie was based on a true story that took place in Italy, and concerned a dog, originally named Ragu, who loved to take long, solitary trips on trains. Eventually Ragu became famous all over Italy, the subject of three separate articles in

Italian popular magazines and finally the star of a best-selling book by her owner, a humble stationmaster in a small town who alternately worried over her whereabouts and basked in the sun of his pet's fame.

The script I wrote changed the setting from Italy to the American West, and the stationmaster to a young boy whose father had been killed while protecting the settlement from Indians, and whose mother then had married a vicious alcoholic captain only because he was the first person who had spoken to her as his troop returned with the arrow-studded body of her late husband. The original ending of the book, where the dog, old and deaf, lies asleep on a railroad track and fails to hear the train, I kept, with the twist that the train is carrying his owner, the former boy, Josh, now grown, back from Harvard where he's just graduated on a full scholarship. The picture made my reputation.

My second film, also a Disney venture, was about a cat who has been part of a laboratory experiment to discover a hormone thought to have great potential in law enforcement, one which would force its recipient into an immediate state of immobility. The cat (named Stan) escapes as one of the researchers accidentally injects himself with the drug, but because there are still traces of the hormone in Stan's small body, the whole rest of the movie and the desperate search to get him back is made even more dramatic because the viewer never knows when Stan will suddenly be unable to move away from a hungry coyote, an oncoming car, or a horned owl.

The film was a tremendous sensation, in part because the animal who played Stan had an unusually engaging personality, but also because of the great outcry from groups which supported using animals for laboratory experiments. Theaters everywhere became the sites for pitched battles between mothers dragging whining children behind them and pickets holding "Right to Experiment" placards and signs, vividly depicting photos of happy children next to the dogs and chimps and cats who gave up their lives for them.

It was during one such showing, in fact, that a distraught woman, waving a picture of a wounded soldier juxtaposed with a goat who had been shot several times so as to better study the treatment of bullet damage, angrily, though probably by accident, managed to plunge the stick on which this diptych was displayed straight into my left eye, not only causing a great deal of pain but blinding me temporarily as well. The woman was taken off by the police and I was treated, only to learn later from a concerned social worker who took the trouble to track me down to discuss her client's case, that my attacker had been none other than Monica, my brother Dave's first love, now confused and under stress from the recent breakup of her marriage, but also possibly responding in a subconscious manner to the resemblance between my brother and me.

Monica and I met in the office of the social worker and, after reaching an initial understanding, went to lunch where I explained the animal rights position. At my apartment, during a private showing of *Stan's Story*, which she admitted never having seen, during the part where Stan meets a giant boa constrictor and is unable to flee, Monica broke into tears and I consoled her.

And so I live now with Monica and her three children, having moved to a fabulous Tudoresque mansion far above the San Fernando Valley of Los Angeles. On nights such as this I can look out over the edge of our spacious grounds and see beneath me the ropes of whitish lights made by thousands of drivers on their way to convenience stores and all-night pharmacies. It's a beautiful effect. Behind me, wandering somewhere through our home, already dressed to attend a daring production of *La Boheme* in which the occupation of Mimi has been changed from a flower-maker to a girl who works in a factory where she rolls cigarettes, Monica is waiting. To my right is our Olympic-size swimming pool, and reflected in its quietly wavy surface are the few stars that have managed to poke their way through the interference of the city's lights.

Who was it who first said, "To be or not to be"?—a statement that's still true, and certainly, life would have been different for me if I'd succeeded in that suicide attempt those many years ago. But are we anything more than just a shopping bag for experiences? I can't answer. To those who ask, however, I say remember this: that birds originally were dinosaurs, and where once there were only conifers on this planet, today acres of rainforests are being destroyed at an incredible rate, a topic, by the way, that will be the focus of my next feature, *Lumamba!*, the story of a baby ocelot, to be filmed in the jungles of Brazil. I remember that many years ago an old cowboy—Billy, I think his name was—told me, "Jim, travel slow and travel light." And though sometimes I've done it and sometimes I haven't, still I have to say at least it's possible.

A DISTANT VIEW OF HILLS

I think it was a gloomy Tuesday evening when I lay down once again to stroke a strand of Marsha's long, dark hair and thought of how she'd cut it off just a few weeks earlier, following that incident involving an overhead fan in a not-so-good-but-still-expensive French restaurant located in one of the farther suburbs of Los Angeles, where I was living.

"Here," Marsha had said, "you take it. You're the one who always liked it so much," and with those words she walked out of my life.

But why was she so angry at me, I asked myself. I wasn't the one who picked that particular restaurant, or even chose that particular table beneath the ceiling fan, though come to think of it, I was the one who spooned the extra sauce onto her *lapin rôti* spilling just a bit down the front of her generously cut dress, causing her to leap from her chair straight into the whirling blades above her head. Even so, later, on our mostly silent drive back home, Marsha had to admit that it wasn't so much the actual heat as the idea of heat in general that had bothered her.

As a result, now I was alone, just another Mr. Lonely Guy like so many other Mr. Lonely Guys, in my black and white wing-tips, my pleated midnight blue pants and white conga shirt, ready to roam the streets and byways of our city in search of romance and perhaps a friend.

The night was overcast. I could feel the beginnings of a light drizzle as I found myself near the center of the city at a private club I knew of called the Peaceable Kingdom. What was unusual about the Peaceable Kingdom was that, once accepted as a member, each patron after entering was expected to choose the animal mask he or she would wear, and then keep it on for the entire evening. Indeed, to remove it, even for something as awkward as a sneeze, was to risk expulsion by the bouncer, a large man (I'm assuming it was the same person each time) wearing the mask of a rare black rhino. The club offered a variety of species to choose from, but I found that most of the regulars, like me, after a few times of experimentation soon settled on one favorite mask for every visit. I had begun as a horned owl, for example, then tried out a panther, then a tiger, but finally settled for a jackal. And the same pattern was evident in others as well, so that far from being, as one might expect, a place of majestic beasts and exotic creatures, most evenings the place was inhabited by a group of happy squirrels, a few rabbits, and maybe even a rat or two. Elephants, lions, bears and so on were usually the mark of a newcomer.

The cuisine of the Peaceable Kingdom was both simple and ingenious. For those wearing the heads of rodents or her-bivores, the club offered a variety of vegetarian dishes—wilted greens spiced with a touch of garlic, a tray of fresh alfalfa sprouts sprayed with a mist of lemon, nuts in a light cream sauce, even peeled avocados on a stick, each football-shaped treat studded with crystals of rock salt. As a jackal, my own favorite dish was tiny frankfurters done up as field mice, with wisps of dill for whiskers, little wedges of bacon for the ears, and for a tail a single chive that was stout enough to allow a diner to pick it up and drop it down his throat.

That night the club was quiet. A herd of Guernseys were grazing in a corner, and several rabbits were whispering into one another's ears at the bar. I sat at a booth in front of a reproduction of the club's namesake, the famous Quaker ideal depicting lions and lambs curled up together. In this version, however, the artist had also included giant carrots, tomatoes, and tree-like stalks of celery, so the question of who got what to eat was even more of a puzzle. In my booth, overcome by a sudden wave of loneliness, I wept quietly into my mask and then, pulling myself together, ordered several field mice and a half-dozen chicken hearts.

I had finished all but one of the delicious mice and was poking at the hearts when I saw her—by whom I mean a female jackal looking around as if this were her first time in the club. I invited her to join me, and suggested she try the remaining mouse. She did, and responded by ordering a half-dozen more, and whether there was magic in the air, or just some mysterious toxic chemical leaking from the freshly laid carpeting that caused two strangers to become more than friends, I'll never know. Her name was Belinda ("It means 'beautiful' in Spanish," she said), and later that night, we watched from her comfortable queen-size bed a rerun of an episode from one of my favorite television shows, *The Swamp of Time*, in which Uncle Jed, his pirogue crushed by the charge of a bull alligator so that he is unable to perform his daily routine of helping maimed and dying wild animals, learns, by way of compensation, the pleasures of settling down in his cabin with a good book.

Belinda said that she enjoyed the show, but confessed she couldn't get all those animals dying without Uncle Jed out of her mind. Probably, she ventured, it was because she herself was a travel agent who specialized in tours for the terminally ill. She had, she said, "a great deal of sympathy for their situation," and explained that her agency, Sunset Travel, had made quite a name for itself by arranging for nurses, medical support, and even "relocation experts," a name she used for those whose job it was to silently and swiftly dispose of any fatalities along the way ("we call them 'sidetrips,'" she said), with minimum disturbance to the others on the tour.

"They like to see ruins," she told me. "Also the biggest and the tallest and the oldest—that kind of stuff. I guess if they think they've seen the best, or whatever, they feel like they can skip everything that led up to it." Belinda paused as she rearranged a false eyelash which had crazily plunged into one eye. "Tell me about *your* last vacation," she said.

I thought for a moment. Before my last vacation I had

written letters to several parts of the country asking the owners of various resorts to describe a typical view that might be seen from one of their rooms. I had been, I wrote, "in the city too long," and had decided that what I needed was a change of scenery. Most of the replies were cursory—the usual illustrated brochure, a list of rates, and an occasional wistful scrawl, "Hope to see you," in the same broad, purple ink favored by PTA committee members and doctors' receptionists. The note that caught my attention, however, was none of these. It was simply a few lines, penciled in a sort of painful, sixth-grade hand on lined paper apparently torn from a pad with spirals along the topmost edge, and, misunderstanding my request, it described the view not from a guest's room, but from the place where the person was writing. "There is a sort of farmyard here," it said, "and I'm looking at a wheelbarrow which has a kind of glazed or frosted look because we've just had a little rain. And next to it are some leghorns, and in the back there is a distant view of hills."

The Bar-H Dude Ranch consisted of the main ranch house, three small cabins, a stable with two horses (Blacky and Whitey), and of course a farmyard, complete with chickens. (The wheelbarrow had been moved or perhaps stolen.) "Howdy," said the grey-haired peculiarly featured woman who greeted me on my first day. "I'm the widow Harkens and this" (she pointed to an aged man in faded denims) "is Gramps. There's no other guest right now but you."

That night, after a roast chicken dinner, I fell asleep. I was exhausted, so it wasn't until well after midnight that I was awakened by the sounds of what seemed to be large animals moving just outside the walls of my cabin, which unfortunately had no windows at all, so I was unable to sneak up and see what sort of creatures they were. I say "animals," but in truth they made a curious shuffling sound, almost as if they were walking on two feet instead of four. I lay there in the dark, not knowing what to expect, and then as suddenly as they had come they shuffled off, leaving me alone.

The next morning, over scrambled eggs, when I mentioned the events of the night before to the widow, she explained that the noises had been made by rats, which found the foliage at the edge of my cabin to be a favorite hiding place. "Don't worry," she said. "Everything sounds bigger at night." Still, after breakfast, curious to inspect the spot where the mysterious noises had occurred, when I looked outside my cabin, not only was I surprised to find that there was no foliage to speak of, but the dirt itself had been swept clean.

The rest of the day was glorious. I sat in an aluminum lawn chair, much as Uncle Jed himself when he found himself pirogueless, passing the time reading and occasionally looking up at the distant view of hills. Oddly enough, Gramps informed me with a sort of swaggering manner I found inexplicably offensive, the hills were not so distant after all, but because of a combination of factors, both vegetal and atmospheric, they only appeared to be. They were, in fact, no more than a few miles away, a ride of a couple of hours at most. I decided that the following day I would pack a lunch, saddle either Blacky or Whitey, and make the trip to see the hills myself. That night after dinner I turned in early, and if there were any sounds outside my cabin I have to say I didn't hear them.

And so the next morning, after a breakfast of three eggs over easy, a bowl of Frosted Flakes, a slice of melon and several homemade biscuits, I saddled up one of the horses and set off toward the hills. It was another perfect day—sunny, with the temperature in the low sixties and a slight breeze from the north. As Gramps, who had looked unusually fatigued over breakfast, had predicted, it didn't take long before I reached the hills. Leaving my horse tied to a stunted tree, I climbed up a couple hundred yards to where there appeared to be an entrance to a long-abandoned mine, and I suppose from that point on you can guess the rest: The mine turned out to be a secret laboratory; Gramps, far from being the senile old codger I had initially supposed, turned out to be an internationally known scientist, notorious for his experiments that involved splicing together the genes of humans and animals (his most perfect creation so far being the widow Harkens). I managed to stumble over a pile of loose rock, there was a shout, a cry, a discovery, and then a struggle between us in which a lantern got knocked over, some smoke, fire, the cries of Gramps as he saw his life's work go up in flames, the screams of his helpless creations, my own hoarse coughs as I crawled slowly toward the entrance, clutching the stirrups, pulling myself up into Whitey's saddle, and then, back at the Bar-H, putting the widow, who had reverted into inconsolable howling, out of her pain with a couple of quick blasts from the shotgun kept around for chicken hawks.

"Wow, that sounds *so* interesting," Belinda said, and told me how, coincidentally, on her last tour, she had taken a group to an obscure natural wonder in the southwestern United States called the Bat Cave, believed to hold the largest concentration of little brown bats in the entire world. "Once inside the cave," she continued, "the stench of the guano was overwhelming. The acridity of the droppings (this being the greatest unmined concentration of such nitrates on earth) made it impossible to breath except by clasping handkerchiefs over our mouths and nostrils, and even so, one middle-aged tourist, Mr. Kessler, who had been suffering from acute kidney failure, fainted dead away and we had to leave him for the relocation experts, who were already complaining bitterly and demanding time-and-a-half pay.

"We pressed ahead," she continued, "to where, thanks to a draft of air from an underground river, the smell abated. Moving forward, often on our knees and hands, at times having to drag some of the weaker members of our party by means of ropes tied under their arms, working in total darkness except for what was illuminated by our special miner's lamps, at last we reached our main destination, an immense cavern that had apparently been the center of some ancient Indian rituals, its walls decorated with strange pictures of half-human, half-animal forms—coyote men and bird women, elk and snakes with human heads, and at times the figures of people who instead of a hand might have an antelope's hoof, or a crow's wing for an arm. The entire ceiling was smooth, like the inside of a skull, and we wondered aloud how those artists whose work was displayed at or near the very top of this gigantic cavern could have drawn it there without our seeing the evidence of great ladders or platforms. Mr. Shanberg, a retired geologist with hardening of the arteries, speculated that at one time the cave may have been filled with water, and the artists had sat in boats as they completed the topmost and therefore oldest work.

"So there we were, staring awestruck at the still-fresh power of those ancient drawings, when suddenly all three carbide lamps, none of which had ever even once failed in any circumstance, sputtered and went out, leaving us plunged in utter darkness. There was a moment of silence, then an awful animal moan. When at last the lamp was relit, I saw Mr. Le Donne, the retired host of a television science show for children, lying face down on the ground, his body horribly mauled by I knew not what, his hand clutching a piece of reddish-brownish fur or hair. Then the light went out again. There was another scream, and when it came back on there was the body of Miss Ketterer, a former high school composition teacher who was living out the last of her days the tragic victim of 'white lung,' a condition brought about by diagramming too many sentences on chalky blackboards. She too had been mauled nearly beyond recognition, and was clutching, even as she might have held a pointer or eraser in her former occupation, a fistful of that same reddish hair.

"'We have to get out of here,' remarked a doctor from Milwaukee who had an advanced case ('self-diagnosed,' he told us proudly) of cirrhosis of the liver.

"'Yes,' replied an accountant from St. Paul who just earlier that day had repaired his malfunctioning pacemaker using only a borrowed paper clip and four feet of dental floss."

Belinda paused. "The rest is pretty much as you'd guess," she said. "We made it to the entrance without further mishaps, but by the time the relocation crew returned to the cave the bodies were gone. Not only that, when we reported our stories to the police we were slapped with a hefty fine for entering a wildlife sanctuary, and the entire case was dismissed under the category of some sort of mass hallucination, which was not surprising given the state of most of those left on the tour, one of whom, Mrs. Loach, took an unscheduled 'sidetrip' even before we could get back to the motel."

I lay back and thought about Belinda's story. Was there, I wondered, some common theme beginning to emerge? This whole strange tale, I recalled, had begun with me in my apartment, stroking what was left of Marsha's hair, and then later on those people in the cave Belinda described had also been clutching hair. Now that I thought of it, the widow Harkens seemed unusually hirsute as well, and of course I had later found out why. I turned to look at Belinda lying next to me. Her hair was short, blond, and very clean. Somehow, the puzzle had yet to be solved.

I remembered my first dog, Rusty, an Irish setter with an uncanny ability to know what was on my mind. His fur, too, had been a reddish brown. At times the expression on his intelligent face was almost human, and no more so than when I would come upon him unexpectedly, sitting before an open library book, staring at what doubtless to him must have been only rows of strange black marks across the page.

What other hair had figured in my life, I wondered. Certainly, when I was young, growing up in the depressive chill of Cleveland, Ohio, in winters and often into spring, my mother used to wrap me in scarves of wool from head to foot before she sent me off to elementary school, a progressive institution which was supposed to help prepare us for life by assigning each student small tasks which would make the larger ones we would have to take on as adults seem more familiar. For the youngest students, the school had a room where pupils addressed envelopes or pasted labels on bottles of shoe polish and paint remover. For the older ones, there was a small art studio, a vegetable garden as well as a tailor shop, and a miniature abattoir, designed for animals up to the size of rabbits.

That's where I was assigned to work, stripping the skins of rabbits as they came off the assembly line at a rate of fifty an hour. If by any chance we fell behind in our quotas (because quotas were a major part of the adult world we would be entering) we were forced to attend long sessions during which we were required to creatively visualize, while kneeling in a corner spread with walnut shells, those emotions responsible for interfering with a smooth and efficient operation, and to banish them. After the skins were removed they went to the school tannery, and from the tannery to the tailor shop where they were sewn into jacket collars or made into muffs for little boys and girls. The worst part of my job came when the rabbits, as often happened, hadn't been killed properly, but only stunned, so were still twitching and making pathetic mewing sounds in front of me even as production quotas forced me to go on with the process. "Thank you," I creatively visualized them mewing as they bid a skinless farewell down the line. "Thank you very much." Still, when by the fourth grade I'd graduated to the tailor shop, despite its poor light and stifling atmosphere, I confess I was glad to have a new job.

Eventually Rusty grew old and his hair began to drop away in patches, and I would gaze at him as he lay in a spot of winter sun or thumped his tail when I walked by. Did he, I wondered, know he was going to die? Or for that matter, what were those rabbits really thinking, their round eyes wide, their little voices squealing on the way to the disemboweling room? What was Rusty's pain to mine? What was his pain to the rabbits'? Was the recognition of pain something only a human soul was capable of? So we were told each day during the school's meditation hour, and curiously enough, once, years later, when I was asked along with the other members of my therapy group to describe my soul, I found myself agreeing with most of the others that it was approximately the size of my own body (though for some it was larger, like a loose-fitting coat, with room to grow, while for others it was slightly smaller, possibly anticipating some future loss of weight). Did this therefore mean that if the souls of rabbits were smaller they felt less pain? If so, then what about those creatures larger than ourselves—a woolly mammoth or a dolphin or a gorilla? Did they feel more? My own theory was that perhaps it had to do with hair, that fur somehow mitigated between us and the world, and possibly the resulting fuzziness made for an easier transition from the self to some far greater other.

"How does a haircut make you feel?" I asked Belinda.

"I like it," she said. "Short hair makes me feel free, and somehow more in touch with everything. Listen, morning's here. What do you say we grab some breakfast and then spend the day at the zoo?"

Breakfast was a leisurely affair—we went out to a cozy country cottage complete with chintz curtains and china coffee cups, soft-boiled eggs from free-range hens, fresh fruit, French rolls, and free refills of fig preserves, but the zoo was a disappointment. Those animals present who were not hiding in the foliage or behind the walls of their dens ("private time" the printed sign in front of each cage described it) seemed unusually somber, mostly staring off with expressions devoid of any alertness or hope whatsoever, similar, in fact, to those on the faces of my fellow citizens of Cleveland, creatures who were only killing time, and who, though they knew not what awaited them, obviously had decided that anything would be better than their present state. The zoo that day had mercifully few visitors—a few children with their distracted mothers, an occasional pair of lovers (though what sort of inspiration for a future life they hoped to find was beyond me), and one solitary man in a white coat, like a lab jacket, tossing health-food muffins to the gorillas. "Health food," I thought. "Right."

The rest of what happened that day you probably have already guessed. Namely, that while heading toward the exit we were accosted by what appeared to be a giant panda. Clearly, I thought, here was a creature who had escaped from whatever compound he had been staying in and meant trouble. And was it my fault if, as it was later explained to me, no such actual panda existed at the time of my sighting, but such a creature *had* once lived there, originally a present from a zoo in mainland China, and as a result had been chosen as the official logo of the zoo? Unfortunately, only a few months after a massive publicity blitz complete with T-shirts, posters and flags using the panda had been undertaken, the poor creature expired after eating several cartons of bamboo shoots containing lethal doses of MSG brought by the well-meaning owner of a local Chinese restaurant. And so, in order not to lose the valuable momentum already generated by the publicity, the zoo had kept the panda (Mao-Mao) as its logo, and simply replaced the actual late animal with a person whose job it was to walk around the park wearing a panda suit and greet visitors.

All this, however, as I have said, was unknown to me as I turned suddenly that Wednesday to see the nearly extinct, but nonetheless largish creature approaching Belinda and me. I went into my "panic mode." Running up behind the imitation-panda, I picked up a nearby two-by-four and struck the creature on its head, disregarding its pathetic cries as well as what I understand now were the well-intentioned efforts of several passersby, who I also attacked as they attempted to explain the difference between a real panda bear, normally a docile creature in its own right, and the unfortunate human being inside the suit whose life I wound up taking.

But all that was in the past, years ago really, even though I must add it still seems like only yesterday when, following our group therapy session at the State Hospital for the Criminally Insane nestled among the golden rolling hills of Atascadero, California, my therapist, Dr. Wolf, told me he had an "interesting proposition" to present to me.

"I have noticed," Dr. Wolf continued, giving a tug to the lobe of his right ear, a nervous trait I had seen worsening in the months that I had been there, "that your responses to the entire series of psychological tests I've given you indicate a strong obsession with and simultaneous fear of things underground. Caves and caverns, for example, are prominent in all the landscapes you have produced in your Art as Healing workshop, but never attics or bell towers." He smiled, baring what seemed to be an unusually large set of teeth.

"Therefore," he said, picking at one of the tiny scabs that had been forming in increasing numbers along the tops of his hands, "I'd like to try an experiment. I propose that you be taken to the basement of this very institution where you will stay in a special cell, attended by our staff, for a full two months, at the end of which I predict you will be completely cured and able to be released again into society."

I agreed. Who wouldn't?

"Oh, and one more thing," he added, fidgeting slightly as he tied and untied his left shoelace. "If I am correct that the source of all your antisocial behavior is simply that your biological clock has been wound too tight, you will have to spend the entire time in the dark. You will not see me or any of the attendants, nor will there be any light for anything down there. Do you agree?"

"OK," I said. "When do I start?"

"Tomorrow," he replied, and hurried out the door. The following day I was led down the stairs to the basement where I was shown, with the last light I was supposed to see for the next eight weeks, the small room where I was to make my home. It was barely tall enough for me to stand, and if I put out my arms I could almost touch the walls, which appeared to be made of reinforced concrete. The floor, curiously enough, had been left as dirt and smelled of urine even though it was perfectly dry. The room, I was told, had originally been built back in the early days of the institution for one special patient, some sort of an artist and a member of an old American family who, after murdering his sister in a ghastly manner, had developed an extreme sensitivity to sounds of all sorts, and thus had to be removed from the general wards above him. My attendants said good-bye, leaving behind a tuna sandwich, a jug of water, and a few utensils to contain my future bodily excretions.

It was, at the risk of repeating myself, dark, and not just any nighttime deprivation, but an atmosphere so thick, so impenetrable, so total, it had a presence all its own. This was not just darkness, I thought, but its essence. Above me I could hear the faint cries of my fellow patients, and around me the humming of the pipes and ducts that were the veins and arteries of the institution. But most of all I heard my own breathing, loud and rather fast, probably from nerves. If I slept, I reasoned, then when I woke the transition from dark to dark would not be so startling and I would accept it more easily. Fortunately the bed and bedding were both comfortable enough so that almost as soon as I pulled the blanket beneath my chin and shut my eyes (a ridiculous gesture if there ever was one) I fell into a dreamless slumber.

I was awakened by someone shaking my bed with persistent and unaccustomed violence. I opened my eyes, and seeing nothing, yelled, "Hey, you!" I jumped up; to my amazement the floor was shaking as well, and then I realized what was happening! As you no doubt have already guessed, we were in the midst of a major earthquake, maybe even "the big one" that had been talked about for so many years for the state of California.

Above me there was a tremendous crash, the sound, I realized, of the entire hospital collapsing, and it was only the fact that I had been put there in the basement, surrounded by these reinforced walls, that had saved my life, at least temporarily. I noticed it was impossible to stand (the ceiling of my cell had been driven down at least a foot by the impact of the collapse) and I could hear the sound of creaking beams, a few horrible human cries which gradually died out, and then a silence that was the most terrifying I had ever felt. My life had been spared, but for what? Yes, I had a little food, and more water, but it was likely I would starve to death before any rescue worker dug his way to me. In the meantime, I could do nothing. The best plan, I decided, was to go back to sleep, not only to pass the time but also to conserve energy.

How long I slept that second time and what dreams I had I cannot say, but I awoke in a sweat to the sounds of my own breath, my own heartbeat, and possibly, I thought, one other thing. In the midst of that profound darkness it seemed I could hear sounds, like voices. My first guess was that some still-playing radio had survived the quake, but then I noticed they appeared to be coming not from above but from the dirt beneath my feet. I put my ear to the ground. The voices, though I couldn't understand their words, were clearer. I tried to remove some of the dirt floor with my fingers, but with little effect because it was so packed. I moved to try another area, and as I did I heard my foot strike some object made of metal, a spoon as it turned out, and I used it to scrape away the hard-packed surface until I reached a layer beneath it that was softer and easier to remove.

How long I worked and how often I rested I have no idea. My guess is that I had lapsed into a time all its own, not a human time but one of space and distances. The dirt was surprisingly loose once past the surface of the floor, and work went easily, but on the other hand I had no idea exactly how long the tunnel I was creating would need to be. Certainly there was no point in tunneling upward, I thought, until I was outside the perimeters of the tons of concrete above me, and because I had no idea where in relation to the institution's walls my basement room had been located, I decided to go in the direction of the voices. The dirt, of course, was a problem, and as my basement room filled, little by little, it occurred to me that, like some strange creature doomed by his own excrement, once the room was full, because the room was the source of my oxygen, I would asphyxiate myself.

Luckily, even as my former cell was reaching its capacity, I began to notice that the wall I was scraping away on seemed to have an increasingly drumlike quality, as if beyond it there were some great hollow space from which these voices emanated, and that the voices themselves were growing louder. I would dig a little, listen, then dig a little farther. The air in the tunnel was stifling, and the heat grew more intense. Even so, once I had gotten within striking distance of my goal I began to hesitate. What, I wondered, would my reaction be if I were a member of some group of cave-dwelling criminals and suddenly my living room wall burst open and someone tumbled through? Moving forward by inches, I brushed away the dirt from the farthest wall with my fingers until I could see a few isolated particles of light passing through it. Then, very carefully, using the handle of my spoon, I removed just enough dirt so I could have an eyehole, a place to peer out at what was on the other side.

The space I looked into was large, and divided by a line of fire shooting out of holes in the rocky floor like flames from an artificial fireplace log. Scattered around the floor on one side of the fire were several apparently random but miniature objects: a table, a chair, a horse, a deer, a lion, an avocado, a pail, a man, a woman, and so on, none of them higher than about half a foot. I looked more closely. The chair was perfect; so were the table, the horse, the man, the woman, the avocado. Clearly these were not just random generations of these forms, but the ideal one of each. Not only that, but the voices which I had heard coming from the opposite side of the fire were speaking what was almost certainly ancient Greek. I pulled back from my vantage point, stunned. As impossible as it seemed, I could come to no other conclusion than that I had somehow stumbled upon Plato's Cave.

I looked again. Around the cave were scattered at least a thousand of these perfect forms: a miniature cow, a full-size screwdriver, a book of matches from some bar, a pencil, a set of towels and matching washcloths, an owl, etcetera, but each living thing, including the human couple mentioned earlier, seemed oddly listless, as if they were under the influence of some unknown narcotic which kept them in a state of nearly suspended animation.

And then I saw behind all of them a thing so peculiar, so *indescribable* (even as I'm pretending to describe it), so absolutely indefinable that even such a detail as its size, for example, became open to debate, as it appeared simultaneously to be the size of a modest living room couch and at the same time so huge that I could scarcely believe there was room for even one other object in the cave, and yet it was both these things. And parts of it were green, the result of various plant-like appendages (I remember what looked like prairie grass, cabbage, artichokes, several pine cones, a dozen or so morels, and broad flat leaves like those of figs), while other parts were as brightly colored as flowers, *were* flowers—blue and yellow and violet in spots—while still other areas seemed to glisten with scales, to shine with feathers, and to be smeared with reddish fur, long in places, short in others, merely bristles. Still other sections were just raw pink skin, which here and there dissolved into tumorlike configurations of cells spilling all around, and there were mouths and ears, and if not eyes exactly, then some things that reminded me of eyes, and some of the plants were turning brown and dying while others were in bloom or bud, and this thing was eating the whole time, though I couldn't say what, and simultaneously defecating, and sweating, while other parts were soaking up the sweat and the excrement, and there was the hiss of escaping gas, and the crunch of bones, and parts of the thing seemed to be inserting themselves into other parts and were throbbing while other parts were crawling forward and yet other ones retreated to the back of the cave (but remember this thing, whatever it was, took up the whole cave, and so had nowhere to move) and from somewhere, I can't be sure where, a high-pitched whine (which either had just started or had been there all along and I'd just missed it) was emanating, and meanwhile, as this was happening, there were coming from it, spewing out from various places in little arcs onto the ground all around it, more of these perfect forms—a stapler, a rabbit, a pair of dress shoes with wing-tips, a swarm of bees, a camera—because, and of course I had known this all along without knowing it, it was the source of all those things and more. And then (and I don't know how to say this either, because I've already said it had no eyes) it *saw* me, saw the tiny shining dot that was the reflection of my eye as it peered through the hole I had made in the wall of the cave, and the resulting shock of, what—desire!, both it for me and me for it—was so intense I found myself thrown back from my vantage point in the dark, back into the body of my tunnel, sweating and staring once more at the tiny hole in all that darkness, gasping, knowing I no longer had a choice in the matter, and that no matter what happened, what would happen, I was about to break through the remaining barrier of dirt to confront whatever beautiful and monstrous thing might be there waiting for me.

I felt a shudder through my body, and then another. I sat back and waited for it to subside, then realized it wasn't coming from my body at all—it must have been an aftershock from the earlier giant quake. I took a breath, and curled into a ball in the hope I might trap as much air as possible around me, and then I lost consciousness.

There was a light, and I found myself staring at a name tag that read, "Hi, my name is BOB." I noticed that the "Hi" part had been printed earlier, and the letters B-O-B had been added later, in purple marking pen, and were followed, probably because its writer had noticed there was still room left, with the symbol of a happy face. I looked at the name-tag owner's head, and the mouth in it opened to say, complete with little puffs of breath around each word, "Hi, my name is Bob." Then it grinned at me. I had been rescued.

I brushed off the dirt, was given a plate of scrambled eggs and a cup of coffee. Except for a couple of visitors, long since gone, who had been necking in the hospital's parking lot at the time of the quake, out of all the patients and all the staff of the State Hospital, I was the sole survivor. Perhaps it was the general confusion, or perhaps having seen too many television shows depicting the criminally insane as slobbering psychopaths of hulking size and threatening demeanor, my rescuers were convinced by my calm responses that I was who I said I was: a mere custodian who, following a nasty spill of toxic glaze in the Self Images in Clay class, had gone down to the basement for a new supply of paper towels to mop the stuff up. So I was able to leave the State Hospital behind forever, much as Dr. Wolf had earlier predicted, although in a completely different way.

Back in Los Angeles, I now live quietly, working days for the county as an Animal Technician II, where it's my job to drag unwanted dogs and cats into the gas chambers where they are put to sleep. For enjoyment I take several creative writing classes, where I write the stories of my life disguised as "exercises," and every so often I return to the Peaceable Kingdom in the hopes of seeing Belinda again, perhaps after her harsher memories of our "date" (as she described it to the court) at the zoo have faded. Once inside the club's comfortable surroundings I put on one mask or another—a gopher or a mole, it no longer seems particularly to matter—and sit watching the door where she might enter.

One evening a few weeks ago, after I'd nearly given up all hope, I saw a woman in the mask of a hyena walk in, and I invited her to my table. After the usual talk and an eclectic cuisine, we wound up back at her apartment, where we watched a show called *Trapper Tom*, a replacement for *The Swamp of Time*, which had apparently succumbed to its miserable ratings. This new show was about a modern mountain man who caught wild animals for a living, and took their skins to town to sell in order to support his favorite charity, a hospital for children, on whose board he sat. Tom divided his time between running down antiseptic corridors full of screaming children—a pelt-covered figure still sticky with the blood of badgers and raccoons—while on his way to solving another medical crisis, and on alternate weeks, returning to the mountains where, covered with pelts and gore, he would rescue stranded, distraught campers and help fight natural disasters. The episode we watched that evening, for example, involved a man and a woman stuck in a cave who could be rescued only after Trapper Tom first caught and uncoiled a gigantic cottonmouth, lowering it to the unhappy couple to use as a rope.

After it was over we sat back in bed and talked a while. Her name, she said, was Linda ("Beauty itself," she explained). We did a little of this and some of that, then she told me the story of who she was and how she came to be at the club, and later, when she took off her clothes, she was nothing at all like I thought she would be.

NIGHT NURSE

I had been sitting trapped in the veterinarian's office with my parrot, Jimbo, waiting to have him treated for the brown and grey mold that was growing at a surprising rate from the base of his beak and on the tips of his wings. There was the usual full house of nervous cats and cringing dogs, but that day the outer room also included an organ grinder whose monkey, Jacques, had apparently developed carpal-tunnel syndrome from having to repeatedly insert his little fingers into his tiny cup in order to dig out the change that provided their livelihood. According to the organ grinder, Luigi, Jacques had been plucked as a baby from a lab that had found a way to reproduce in lower primates certain painful viruses formerly found only in humans, the symptoms of which, shortly before their inevitably fatal denouement, included a mysterious feeling of sadness and a longing for a better life.

Fortunately, Luigi said, Jacques (who had been named after Jean Jacques Rousseau) had been rescued by him and a group of fellow animal-rights activists before the monkey had received the complete series of injections, so although Jacques did exhibit a marked preoccupation with distances, and sometimes in the midst of begging would bury his small head in his arms and sob, most of the worst effects of the disease seemed to have been averted.

A long silence in the waiting room followed this story. Luigi looked around for a moment, then shrugged, a touch self-consciously. "If," he said, "I seem unduly identified with my little pet, it is because his life so closely resembles my own. I was stolen from my own parents, Anna and Giuseppe, many years ago by a well-meaning hippie couple, Sunshine and Tor, who smuggled me out of Italy and into the United States where it became my job to make paper flowers for their religious commune in northern California. From this early employment I rose in trust and responsibility until I was made the head of a team of fellow commune members who canvassed major airports all over the country, persuading jet-lagged travelers to purchase our cellulose blossoms, and it wasn't until I reached the age of thirty that I inexplicably tired of this boring but admittedly secure form of existence.

"One evening at Los Angeles International Airport I went into the men's room and climbed up on a toilet so my feet would not be visible to anyone who might be checking beneath the doors of the stalls for occupants. I shut the stall door and, despite severe leg cramps, remained in that position for as long as I could to avoid detection. Seventy-two hours later, unbelievably stiff but free at last, I climbed back down and became, as you can plainly see, an organ grinder." This time the silence in the waiting room was broken by the persistent scratching of a Labrador, apparently in for a flea problem.

"That is *so* sad," the woman sitting next to me remarked. It turned out she was taking her cat in to be examined for hairballs. ("Thank God it's nothing serious," she said. "I don't know what I'd do without Cinderella.") After making more small talk she invited me to her house that evening for a supper of veal Parmesan, which, she said, she'd prepared earlier, adding, "That's a great parrot you've got there, mister, but you'd better leave him at home." In fact I was glad to do so, never having been a particular fan of parrots, and certainly never picturing myself owning one, let alone taking one to the vet for mold, but neither had I counted on meeting its previous owner, Ginger, one afternoon several years earlier as I wandered the corridors of a New Age convention, looking for some clue to a past life I had been told would explain the feelings of confusion that frequently overwhelmed me as I contemplated this one.

The convention hall was larger than I had thought, and surprisingly disorienting. I had gotten to the point where all

I wanted was to sit down when through an open door I heard a voice, a woman's. She was explaining that the way a person knew he or she was the child of an alcoholic was not so much by the fact that their parents passed out every night at the dinner table but that, when grown, the child would come to trust animals more than people. I sat down.

Her name, as I have said, was Ginger, and she told us that the way she had overcome this problem in her own life was to surround herself with animals so surly, cranky, eccentric and ill-tempered that there was no way anyone could trust them. She specialized in finding dogs who had spent their lives guarding rusting automobiles, mauling Jehovah's Witnesses, or simply acquiring a history of senseless, random acts of viciousness. "I was bound," she said, raising up a shapely though scar-covered forearm, "but now I'm free."

After she had finished her talk I asked her if she wanted to join me for a glass of wine at a favorite haunt of mine, the Cafe de God. (Originally the cafe was to have been called the Cafe de Chien but when a brilliant but dyslexic monolingual artist had created the wrong sign its owners had decided to keep it instead of paying for a new one.) At the cafe we exchanged stories of pet attacks and debated the question of what makes man so special in the first place. Ginger maintained it was our ability to override all existing evidence just to believe that somewhere outside of our lives there is another world, either subsequent or concurrent which, though invisible, explains everything. My own position was that it's only our sense of beauty that separates us from animals. "Consider," I said, "the amount of pleasure we take in sunsets, panoramas, statues, colors, music, mini-malls, etcetera. Does any animal do that?"

"And why should they?" Ginger replied. "They're happy. They don't need that stuff."

Thus we became friends, not close, but close enough for me to be shocked when I received the news that Ginger had been killed one afternoon as she stooped to retrieve a spent

Frisbee which was resting against the side of *PT 54-1/2* (the monumental public sculpture of an authentic World War II PT boat which had been cut exactly in two and filled with memorabilia of the late president John Kennedy, including, controversially, three whole compartments devoted to illustrating various assassination theories). Somehow, due to a defective mooring cable, just as Ginger was bent retrieving her Frisbee, the boat gave a sudden shudder and toppled over. Her death, curiously, was not from broken bones but from drowning, the ground being soft from over-watering that day, and even more surprising was the news that I had inherited, as her last wish, the large, decaying parrot with the name so very similar to mine, this same bird I was currently treating for some as yet unidentified form of fungus.

And what *was* Ginger's message, I wondered. Jimbo was certainly an attractive enough bird, but after all he *was* only a parrot. I wondered if somehow that very fact was meant to function as one last rebuttal from the grave to our very first argument: that all our notions, whatever they may be, simply parrot some greater, higher power.

I am not what most people would call a great reader, nevertheless I do remember once coming across a parable about a traveler who, on the way home from the airport after a long trip, is stopped by a stranger holding up a blank sign.

"What is it you need?" the traveler asks.

"I need nothing," says the stranger.

"What is it you want?" the traveler persists.

"I want nothing," replies the stranger.

"Then why, for God's sake, have you stopped me when I am rushing to return to my family?" the traveler demands.

"It is not my needs I am considering," says the stranger, who it turns out is a robber, "but the needs and wants of those around me, beginning with my children and my wife, and extending to the generations yet unborn."

And with that, the robber stabs the traveler, takes his bloody wallet and his suitcase down to a nearby river, washes off what's salvageable and throws the rest away. Then he carries the loot back to his family, who meanwhile, unbeknownst to him, have been burnt up in a fire caused by one of his children who was playing with a butane cigarette lighter the robber had taken from a previous traveler.

So who *is* responsible for the needs of others? And how far does that responsibility go? Was it my fault that the calves for Martha's (for that was her name) already-prepared dinner of veal Parmesan had been raised in darkness, confined to tiny boxes filled with their own excrement, had never been given the chance to run, to even walk, to see the light of day, or to experience life if only for a minute before they were killed in order that some human wouldn't have to chew as hard? Should I have felt guilty? The calves were long dead, it's true, but on the other hand, I reasoned, new ones would have to be created to fill the void left by Martha's cooking.

And was it my fault that Martha did not know that I was notorious for accepting invitations to dinner and then not showing up, or that, already despondent over the death of Cinderella (who had choked on a hairball on the drive home from the vet), Martha decided that my failure to attend her dinner was the last in a long series of signs that her life in general had gone on long enough, and so killed herself after first leaving behind a note which spelled out in no uncertain terms my culpability in the matter?

It's hard to explain why, but certainly all this was running through my mind as I sat in the nurses' lounge watching my favorite television series, *Angel of Death*, the story of a heroic nurse who goes from town to town administering euthanasia to one lovable and needy patient after another. Each episode tended to build around a disguise, or at least an impersonation that Kelly needed to assume to convince the hospital authorities (or the concerned family) to let her have a few moments with the soon-to-be deceased. Kelly favored, I had noticed, announcing herself as a long-lost child, or sometimes a grandchild, and the dramatic and at times comical effects that followed were the result of her other "siblings" eventually convincing themselves that she had merely slipped their minds.

Needless to say, the success of *Angel of Death* soon led to a host of other "nurse shows," including another of my favorites, *Nightmare Nurse*, which took a more negative approach. In it, a visiting nurse is supposed to go to various patients' homes to care for them so they won't have to go to a hospital. Instead she ties them to large kitchen appliances until they sign over all their bank accounts, has them legally declared senile, and then leaves. As you can imagine, the hero of this series isn't the nurse, but Steve, a doctor recently deprived of his license for selling large amounts of amphetamines without prescriptions, who is trying to worm his way back into the graces of the authorities by performing good deeds of a medical nature, and whether the hapless elderly were still alive at the show's end or had perished from dehydration, my favorite part always came when the doctor turns to the camera and says, "Wherever she is, wherever she may be, she will not escape the vengeance of Dr. Steve."

I first decided to become a nurse when I myself had been in a hospital, friendless and groggy with pneumonia, lapsing in and out of episodes of *I Dream of Jeannie* and *Bowling for Dollars*, my only solace being the cool hands and soothing voices of the hospital staff. I was in the Army then, and in order not to board the plane taking my fellow servicemen to Vietnam, had stood for hours with my feet in an icy creek until I contracted a severe case of pneumonia. One medical complication led to another, and as a result I missed not only that plane, but each one for the next six months until I was discharged at last, my health broken, but my conscience clean.

Luckily so, because I later discovered that the soldiers I was to have gone with had all been slaughtered when someone tossed a bomb inside a crowded theater (showing, interestingly enough, *Nite Nympho Nurse*, a porno flick about a nurse who fornicates her way through every ward of a large metropolitan hospital, ending up on the children's wing—a movie too controversial ever to be shown in the States except occasionally when passed off, because of its extremely dim lighting, as an art film).

I like hospitals and I like the sick, and of all the times that I can be with them, my favorite is the night shift, those hours from eleven to seven, when everyone's asleep. I arrive; I check the charts and see who made it through the day and who did not. I visit them, wish them all sweet dreams, and then I go into the nurses' lounge and wait until the last few restless patients drift to sleep. I'm a night nurse, and I have my orders. As I move along the silent halls I look inside each room to make sure the sleeper's still alive and lying there, his mouth half-open, her limbs half-moving; I watch the beads of sweat along their foreheads' slippery slopes; I note the steady drip of fluid into veins; I mark the wheezes of breath, the gasps for air, the innocence of faces that don't know they're being watched. They are all good then, no matter who they are or what they've done by light of day, impersonal as fish along the shadow of a bank, as touching as a child who'll take a stranger's hand believing that the stranger will take him home again. I have my orders.

I change the I.V. drips, wake some in the middle of their dreams to give them pills they won't remember in the morning, pull covers up, empty out dishes brimming with bile or sputum. And sometimes I'll touch them in a place that finds its way into their dreams; they'll stir, will say a name, and then I say my own name, Jim, back into their ears. By morning I'm gone. It isn't mine to feed them or to give them baths or to speak of getting better. I am the ambassador of the dark, with its sighs, its words, the blackness around the beam of my penlight. I lap like waves past where they are sleeping. I turn, as Whitman writes, but I do not extricate myself.

Or so I used to say. These days I'm a professional bounty hunter, and they call me the Night Nurse for the way I have of putting my quarry to sleep before clamping on the cuffs, although, to tell the truth, it's not that hard, because most of the fugitives I pursue are just like you—tired accountants, scared gamblers, ex-nurses, ex-teachers, ex-preachers, ex-policemen whose only crime was that they were left alone with temptation one time too often; ordinary people, who even in their fleeing, remain exactly as they were before that one act which they'd hoped would separate them from everything that went before—and by the time I track them down all they really want to do is take a break, order a coffee and maybe a glazed donut, to clear the air about their lives once and for all.

And it's not just this wish for normalcy that brings them in but that they're tired—that whatever bookkeeper, or clerk, or treasurer of a flower club they once were, now they are living, thanks to the fear of being discovered, in a state of poverty far worse than anything they had ever experienced. "Five years," they tell themselves, "and I'll be free to spend it." But after five long years of looking around corners and checking the little peepholes on their front doors, the habit becomes engrained. "Another five," they think. "You can't be too safe," so in the end, just before they're apprehended, it's hard to say who is catching whom, and finally the thought of spending a couple of years behind bars, having a couple of legs broken or having a couple of concrete blocks fitted to their feet and being tossed off the side of a boat in the harbor starts to feel almost like a relief.

This was the story with my last case, that of Judy, a simple stenographer for the Central Intelligence Agency who, one day while taking the dictation of a letter to the wealthy head of a vicious reactionary army illegally supported by our government, went bad. The letter indicated that his next payment of a half million dollars in unmarked bills might be picked up in the trash bin of a Dairy Queen near the Beltway. In fact Judy knew the place, having necked there as a teenager, and she was surprised it was still open. Surely, she rationalized, the money, rather than going to a group whose chief activity was the torture, rape and murder of simple farmers, could be funneled to an organization that takes care of those in our own country who had been forced, through the economic policies of the 1980s, to live in the streets or in nursing homes. ("A drop in the bucket," she later remarked to me, "but it would have been *something*.")

Unfortunately, no sooner did she fish out the money from an empty box of hot dog buns than the fear syndrome set in. In order to remove herself as far as possible from her former profession, and maybe also to fulfill a long-repressed fantasy, she became an exotic dancer, rightly assuming that because she was middle aged and the product of a sedentary lifestyle, no one would look for her in such a venue. This turned out to be true, of course, but she forgot it also meant there would be only a few clubs willing to hire her, even on a trial basis, and when one did, more than once she found herself with tears in her eyes, leaving the stage to shouts of "Sit down, Grandma," and threats of bodily harm yelled out by intoxicated executives her own age, unhappy to be reminded of their own sagging flesh.

I tracked Judy down using her charitable instincts as a guide, from a mailing list of the United Way, and took her under custody following a benefit performance she had just given at the Old Seamen's Home in Memphis, Tennessee, where she stripped to traditional dances.

"Does this mean the jig is up?" she asked, her face still flushed with the success of her artistry.

"Yes, Judy," I said. "It does."

Returning home to my apartment after I handed Judy over to the authorities, I was dismayed to find Jimbo dead, lying on his back on the bottom of his cage, his colorful feathers collecting dust, his neck horribly twisted. I couldn't stop imagining the poor bird's last moments: At first curiosity ("A sound! What's that?"), then joy ("Some company! Someone to chat with!"), then puzzlement ("Hey! What's he trying to do?"), then finally, caught with nowhere to go, no place to fly to, his back pressed horribly against the bars of his cage, terror ("No!").

But who could have done such a thing? The doors and windows were all locked; no one could have gotten in, save through the tiny skylight I'd left open a crack for air in the bathroom, but the skylight was too small for a normal human being. Maybe a child could have done it, I thought, but if so how did he leave the apartment? The doors and windows were still locked, and anyone leaving by the skylight would have had to push a table or a chair beneath it in order to climb back out again. The only clue was a small tuft of reddish-brown hair caught at the intersection of two wires of Jimbo's cage. I was and still remain completely baffled.

Removing Jimbo from his fatal, final home, I noticed for the first time the newspaper on which he lay, one I had carelessly snatched from a pile beneath the kitchen sink to line the bottom of his cage. On it was a picture of a starving mother and her child, both lying on the ground, the mother propped up on one elbow, her hand extended, holding out a small bowl for alms. I wiped a tear shed over Jimbo from my eye so as to better read the caption. It simply stated that here was a woman who, along with her child, was lying alongside the road begging for food. The paper was a few weeks old. Did her picture being there help her? I doubted it, and probably she was dead before it was even printed.

Someone, I forget who, once hypothesized that the reason we write is to recreate some moment of pure pleasure from our pasts, some exquisite sensation of oneness or wholeness with the world we associate with a specific time or place—a color, a temperature, a smell. For all of us, the writer wrote, the rest of our lives is simply trying to get back to that sensation. Was that the object behind the parrot's mindless chatter? If so, then was that also the case for me? Finally, if that was true, what was the sensation I was trying so hard to duplicate? Arrogance? Guilt? Boredom? Terror? Or was it only feeling sorry for myself through Jimbo? I searched the faces of that dying woman and her child for a clue, as I search yours now, you, my prisoner, chained to the special ring I've had welded to the frame of my automobile which even now is speeding through the dark as you lie there sleeping in the passenger seat, moving in your dreams and to the motion of the car, incorporating all of this—the music from the radio, my voice as I speak these words to you, your day, your fears, your hopes, as together we head toward some half-dreaded and half-welcomed destination.

GIGI

ғоʀ Michael Roloff

I

We were flying high over the Atlantic ("embarrassingly high," my seat companion had chosen to describe it) just before I dozed off only to be awakened by a crash and the sensation of silently (although I know there must have been an avalanche of air pouring by my unprotected ears) falling directly into the ocean.

Previous to that I had been in Portugal, collecting tapes which I would alter, illegally rerecord on compact discs, and then sell to restaurants. The songs were "fados," traditional and heartrending popular laments similar to the blues, songs about things that were lost or had faded, however unlike the complaints of the blues, these were of a rather specific nature: the death, by cancer of the colon, of a woman with whom the singer had lived for nearly forty years; the loss of an only child in a school bus crash determined to have been caused not by driver error, but by bad brakes; being laid off from a job only a week before the singer would have been eligible for full retirement benefits.

These original tapes I would transcribe, reorchestrate for strings, add a heavier beat, and then have performed by several unemployed musicians of my acquaintance. My reasoning was simple: it was my belief that most people ate not because they were hungry, but to cover up their pain. If I could, in a pleasant way, increase the level of their discomfort, they would eat more. And it seems that I was right. The demand for *Music to Dine By* was so great that following this trip I was planning *Music to Dine By, II.*

I was also in the beginning stages of initiating a new enterprise, to be called *Music to Be Happy By*. The theory behind this concept originated one day when I was driving along the freeway and saw an unfortunate motorist at the side of the road, being written up by a highway patrolman for a ticket. What struck me was not this duo, however, but the happy expressions on the faces of my fellow motorists—they were clearly thrilled. This new project, therefore, was to blend together the cheerful and gregarious native music of some unsuspecting culture with the sounds, extracted from a government training film I had obtained by means I can't divulge, of various prisoners, mostly political, being tortured through the use of the methods the film sought to illustrate. I was cautiously optimistic about the success of this new project as well.

By now I suppose it is a cliché how quickly we, who struggle all our lives, when at last we find ourselves in a situation that is out of our control, arrive at a state of resignation. No regrets, no last messages, no flash of life before our eyes, and certainly, if we've learned anything from countless "black box" recordings taken from past airplane crashes, the mantra of choice when facing imminent death is simply, "Oh shit," followed by a silence. And no doubt this also would have been true in my case, except that falling out of airplanes does provide a little more time for reconsideration, rather like bumping into an old friend at a supermarket, chatting, saying everything you want to, parting, and then having to stand behind him for five minutes in the checkout line, remembering as you do the long list of grudges you also hold against the creep.

Thus, among my descendent thoughts, I found myself imagining (correctly, as it turned out) exactly what had happened. That is: Government A believed that its national honor had been impugned (which, of course, it had) so it decided to teach the impugning government (Government B) a lesson by impugning the honor of the impugning government. The results were familiar ones: Government A felt its honor was restored, while Government B now demanded further revenge, and meanwhile the lives of many citizens in both countries were lost, leaving behind a trail of endless grief, of closets full of dusty clothes, of rooms of abandoned toys, of boxes full of bobbie pins to put up hair that no longer existed; and the world, never the choicest of locations to pitch a life, became a little worse.

As you no doubt have guessed, I survived, but through what must have been the oddest combination of circumstances. First, the section of the plane in which I was dozing somehow must have remained attached to the wing, which, instead of plunging straight down or breaking into pieces, apparently spiraled earthward like a maple leaf (coincidentally, the emblem of my high school back in Ohio), slowing my descent at least long enough, because I had neglected to fasten my seat belt, for me to be thrown from the remnant of the plane completely, at which point I found myself once again awake. Next, I felt a series of bone-shaking collisions, rather like speed bumps taken at two hundred miles an hour, which later turned out to have been several members of a flock of endangered snowy egrets, three of which I found myself still clutching (and to whom I believe I owe my life) when at last I found myself in the center of a bed of moss, remarkably similar to those rubberized blocks one finds in pole vault pits in track meets, in the middle of an island in the Atlantic. To this day I have no idea what happened to my fellow passengers.

I had heard of Amazons, of course—who hasn't heard the legend of that fierce band of women warriors who were said to have had their home somewhere in South America—but before arriving on the island, the only similar experience I had was during the year I had spent as a teacher at the Ladies Preparatory School outside Chattanooga, Tennessee. It was with frequent pleasure that I thought of those independent and self-reliant girls who made up the members of my Egyptian History Study Group: Darlene, and Tara, and Marlene, and LuAnn, and Maureen, and Joline—young girls smelling of fresh soap and jonquils, wearing white dresses with pale blue ribbons for belts, who under my supervision eagerly constructed a twenty-foot-tall pyramid made of discarded Moon Pie wrappers in the field hockey area, and then one by one brought their dead dogs and cats, already mummified according to the strictest Egyptian formulas, to be buried in the center. I marveled at their craftsmanship as they constructed miniature boats to carry the souls of the dead to the other life, admired their calligraphy as they wrote farewell messages to their departed pets in authentic hieroglyphics, and was humbled by their sensitivity as they wept over their furry pals.

Now, two years later, after having been released from teaching duties (for "purely budgetary reasons," the headmistress said, and she added that she had never seen the girls so "fired up"), lying on the spongy peat, gasping, naked, my clothes having been ripped off by the force of air following the explosion, atop a pile of dead egrets, my hearing miraculously restored, I found myself surrounded by a ring of wild, half-clad young women brandishing clubs. I looked up, uncertain as to what would happen next.

"Why, Mister Krusoe," said one of them (Darlene, I think), "we had no idea we would find *you* here!"

Later, back at their cave, after I had been bathed and bandaged, I heard the story of how, returning home from their junior year in Cairo, my ex-pupils suddenly felt their own giant airliner crack in two, as the tail section (in which they had been given adjoining seats) slowly spun, once again like a pod from a giant maple tree, away from the rest of the plane, sparing them, except LuAnn who had been on her way back from the lavatory at the time of the concussion. In her memory the girls had erected a shrine at one end of the cave, with a simple statue of Thoth, the Egyptian god of the dead, built out of bits of driftwood and pieces of seaweed and dressed in the only article of clothing left from LuAnn's life, a "Drive 'Em Wild" garter belt covered with emblems of little red steering wheels that Marlene had borrowed earlier and had been wearing when their plane fell from the sky.

II

It all seemed like a dream, and it was. I woke to find myself on still another island, this one Manhattan, in my Greenwich Village apartment ready to face another day of teaching my course in the Psychology of Sleep at New York University. The day was going to be a difficult one because I knew I could wait no longer to break off my longstanding relationship with one of my students, Gigi. Gigi and I had first met in one of the labs where she was being studied following a freak accident. It seems she'd been lying on the beach in her too-small bikini, sipping a Coke, getting a tan, reading "The Death of Ivan Ilyich," when a stainless-steel rod from an exploding passenger jet dropped straight into her brain. She had experienced a moment of panic, she said, and blinding pain of course, and then simply returned to the part of the story where Ivan is wishing he had a job that brought in just a bit more money.

What was unusual about Gigi was that the rod hadn't affected her normal behavior, and she had come to the sleep lab as a last resort after the physical psychologists could find nothing "wrong" with her. "Gigi," I sometimes used to say in a joking manner, "the only thing that rod must have done was take all the meanness from you," which in fact was true.

Due to the risks inherent in any surgery of such a nature, it was eventually decided to leave the rod just where it was, and so all we did, after sawing off the extra length, was to cover each end with a rubber cap to prevent damage if she banged into things, as she often did. Despite all this, or maybe because of it, Gigi did remarkably well, and only once during the two years of our affair had I noticed any particular discomfort. That was when we were staying in a Howard Johnson's outside of Pittsburgh and Gigi turned suddenly and the exposed end of the cranially located rod, the rubber cap of which had fallen off, struck against the frame of our vibrating bed, which must have had a short. She screamed, attracting the attention of the desk clerk, who promptly gave us another, higher-priced room at no extra charge. On the other hand we *had* discovered through our own experimentation that a tuning fork, attached to one end of her rod, properly struck, could bring about sensations of exquisite pleasure which lasted for hours.

But now, of course, those days were over. It was time for Gigi to begin to think about graduate school, and go off on her own, something I knew she would be unable to do so long as she remained hopelessly in love with me.

III

In real life, as you may have guessed, I never, as in my earlier dream, taught Egyptian history, having been too busy with my studies in psychology, the unconscious, and vivisection to branch out into other areas. On the other hand, it's difficult

106

for me to overestimate the profound impression made on me by a present on my fifth birthday of a genuine Egyptian scarab. This beetle, my aunt explained, was the symbol of the cycle of life, chiefly due to its ability to strip the features from the face of a dead loved one, digest them, use the nutrients, and then have them magically appear again in the form of thousands of baby beetles, covering the walls of the tomb like a large-screen television turned to the wrong channel. It was the size of the picture, she said, that was impressive, and naturally one had to make some sacrifice in quality.

Thus it was that walking into the Cafe Dante, off Washington Square, I immediately spotted Gigi seated at our favorite table near the gutter, despite the fact that something was different about her. She was radiant, clearly excited over some news. I gulped with a sinking feeling. I had a pretty good idea what her news might be, and if I was correct, now, just as I was trying to extricate myself from this relationship, was exactly the wrong time for it to happen.

"Gigi," I said, walking up with a gesture I hoped would convey warmth, yet a certain distance. "You seem very well pleased with yourself this morning."

"Well, yes," she said, and perversely made me order breakfast before she would agree to divulge her secret. A bad sign, I thought.

My food arrived—a double espresso, a bowl of Frosted Flakes, and a small orange juice, the same breakfast I'd been having for years. "Now," I said, with a firm but understanding smile on my face, "tell me your news."

She struck the rubber cap of the rod through her head with a spoon in an involuntary gesture of anxiety. "Well," she said, "do you remember how a while ago you tried to get me to quit smoking because you said it was bad for my health?"

Oh, oh, I thought. Here it comes.

"Well," and she banged the spoon against the rod once again, making a sound like a tiny, muffled bell, "the contest I entered with all the wrappers from those packs of cigarettes is sending the two of us on an all-expense-paid trip to Cairo. We leave in a week; what do you think of that?"

I exhaled. I *was* pleased, and the fact that we would be leaving shortly meant there would be plenty of time left for the vacation, the breakup, and applications to graduate schools. I smiled for a moment as I remembered how often even so-called dream vacations turn into nightmares of togetherness.

I had never seen Gigi happier than in the days before our flight, and I watched with pleasure as she moved in a flurry of dialing weather reports, packing, and buying travel books. Later, it was from just one of those books that she had concluded reading some incredibly tedious statistics to me, when I rose to go to the lavatory on the airliner somewhere over the Atlantic, I suddenly found myself mid-air, no doubt the result of a tremendous explosion. I was alone. The plane was nowhere in sight, and I was falling.

"Bye-bye, Gigi!" I shouted, and pointed my toes in hopes that this would minimize the area of my impact with the sea, the surface of which, I remembered reading once, from the height I was descending promised to be like steel.

To this day I have no idea how I survived the fall. I believe it was the pointed toes that did it (and mine were numb for weeks), or a freak updraft, or just possibly it was only a miracle, pure and simple. In any case, I remember swimming, and then the sound of gentle surf (the same sound as on the nature record I would play to go to sleep back in New York!), and then somehow waking up on shore, surrounded by hundreds of tiny blue crabs, each with eyes on separate stalks, all turned toward me.

After an extemporaneous meal of several of these trusting creatures, raw, I set out to explore what I quickly discovered was an island, and one which was completely deserted, at that. It soon became clear I had been unbelievably lucky in the location of my fall: there was a spring of fresh water, several plants which looked to be and in fact were potatoes, many varieties of edible beans, and, on the opposite end of the island from where I had landed, two huge sections of a cargo plane which must have crashed some years earlier, its contents full of freeze-dried meals, canned fruits and vegetables, matches, a small library, an ample stock of warm clothing, penicillin, paper, pens, and a case of disposable butane lighters, all intact. Considering everything, by my calculations there were enough supplies to last me at least fifteen years, even supposing I took no particular care in rationing them. So I began my life on the island, my days spent in keeping my journal, an incredibly dull affair, even to me. I breakfasted on Belgian waffles, and ate lunches and dinners of Chicken Florentine, Chicken Almondine, and Chicken Stroganoff, arranging the leftover aluminum-lined packets into a gigantic reflecting pyramid.

So went my days. My nights, though quiet, were not much better. Following a freeze-dried dinner (sometimes supplemented by a few dozen crab legs or a tasty fish) I would sit around the campfire (I took care to always build a campfire, just in case some searchers might be passing by at night) and sang the songs I remembered from Boy Scout camp as a youth—"Clementine," and "The Worms Go In" (I don't know if that was its real title), and "A Hundred Bottles of Beer on the Wall," even though Boy Scout camp itself, I must say, had been a hideous affair, a vicious playground for the demonstration of the laws of survival of the fittest, a sinkhole of pleasure and terror, a place where to fall asleep was to expose oneself to being set on fire, to being forced to pee in one's sleep, or just to being the victim of simple buggery. At least on the island, I thought, I could sleep in peace. That is, except for a recurring dream.

In the dream I was, oddly enough, back on the island of that earlier dream, the one with the girls I'd dreamt I'd taught back in high school. There they were again: Darlene, Marlene, and Joline, all standing around wearing compassionate expressions and the skins of small dead animals, stitched together using techniques I imagined they'd learned in Home Ec class.

"Mr. Krusoe," they would smile at me, "just lie still and we'll do everything." Then Joline would produce a loofa and wash my legs, which had gotten quite dirty (and alas, quite abraded) during my fall.

"Ouch!" I would say, and after that the others would lead me to their larder, where I was surprised to see that even under the primitive conditions of their existence they had managed to find adequate substitutes for yeast, flour and butter. Then they would hand me a croissant, saying, "Eat this," and I would, and then, still in my dream, I would fall asleep, and that is what was so unnerving, because never in all my years of sleep research had I ever heard of such a thing as a dream during an actual dream. This frightened me.

On the bright side I imagined the paper I would one day deliver at one of our frequent conventions, usually held, lest you get the idea that we sleep researchers are a free-spending bunch, at an inexpensive chain of motels called Tut's Travel Tombs, where the chief extravagance was a health-inducing pyramid at the top of every Cleopatra-size bed. My paper would be entitled, "Notable Lapses in Consciousness During the Dream State," and I imagined an eventual catalogue of all such occurrences, from catnaps to waking dreams, to actual instances where the dreamer dies, is quiescent for a while, and then finds himself reborn as a lower animal. Dreams such as the latter, I reasoned, could well be behind the sudden interest in those movements, by which our own lab had been plagued, for so-called "animal rights."

Later on I would awake and the girls would comb my

hair, strip off my clothes, and rub my body with a perfumed oil they said they had learned to extract from a local, fragrant seaweed. Then, before any of us would realize how it had happened, the girls and I together would find ourselves coated with the stuff, which carried just the slightest odor of dead crabs, and in no time would be sliding and slipping into each others' orifices in the most delightful and unusual ways. Then, all at once, still dreaming, I would stop. Something would be wrong. One or more of the girls would be missing, a different one each time. "Wait," I would say, "where are the others?"

Uncannily, the remaining girls, whether Darlene or Marlene or Joline, would look at me with absolute sincerity and say, "Why, Jim, there are no others."

IV

Earlier, you may recall, I wrote that Gigi's dreams were normal in every way. The one exception I can now remember took place not in the sleep laboratory, where I had spent so many happy hours gazing at her tossing and turning figure, but in a Best Western Motor Lodge in Moundsville, West Virginia, where we had stopped overnight on the way to visit her parents in Memphis, Tennessee. We were both exhausted, and had barely finished our dinners of chicken-fried steak, mashed potatoes and lime jello, when to ferry us to dreamland we decided to watch a rerun of a show about a man stuck with a cast of strange and curiously nonchalant characters on an island. That night their island became the sanctuary for a gang of international terrorists who took the entire regular cast hostage, until one of them, the hero, snuck off to signal for help. Then, while the hostages remained tied (and the hero himself returned to pretend to be tied along with them), the terrorists were attacked by special forces sent by Interpol who, after a bloody gun battle, defeated the terrorists and flew off without stopping to wonder who might have called

111

for help in the first place. (This of course is my nightmare today, that I could be asleep or on the wrong side of the island when help came by; perhaps, for that matter, it already has—I have no way of knowing.) At the end of the show the hero, after hearing no noise for a few hours, untied his friends who, angered by his forgetfulness, tied him up, constructed a raft out of various empty cans of fruits and vegetables, and left him behind forever. Then Gigi and I fell asleep.

In any case, the dream that followed was remarkable. It began with her dying, Gigi said. "There was a big bang, followed by a lot of white stuff, like feathers, and then it was like being born all over again, but this time in a distant land. You know," she continued, "how sometimes you're in your car at a drive-in movie watching the screen but the sound is really coming from those speakers hanging on the edge of your window? Well, that's what was going on. I mean, there I was, taking care of you because you had hurt yourself somehow, but the person who was me in the dream wasn't exactly me, but it was a younger version who reminded me of a girl in my class back at the Ladies Preparatory School, a sweet girl who smelled of jonquils and pine tar soap, who wore underwear that drove boys crazy, and had a perpetual urinary tract inflammation. So there we were, you lying on your stomach with me giving you a full-body massage, and I had just worked my way to your you-know-what when everything went blank."

"Oh," I said, and then we went to a coffee shop, ate two orders of Pancakes Supreme, and got an early start for Memphis to visit Bill and Lib, Gigi's parents, who hated me even as they feigned not to. The truth revealed itself, however, on the last night of our visit, following a dinner at a Chinese restaurant. We had finished our meals of chicken-fried shrimp and greens and had been through the compulsory reading aloud of fortunes (mine was "You will take a trip") when Bill, in an effort to refill my teacup after I had already told him I didn't want any, managed to drop the entire pot straight onto my handwritten doctoral thesis (in washable blue ink) which I had carried with me for safekeeping, ruining the entire draft. And although I do not blame Bill, however much his subconscious may have desired it, I must admit I never finished my thesis, which had been tentatively titled "Projecting the Future through the Soiled Windows of Unconscious Structures." Not, I suppose, that it would have helped me here on the island.

V

On page 608 of *The Interpretation of Dreams, the Third Edition*, Sigmund Freud finally gets around to what earlier he had just been hinting at. Dreams, he says, are "the royal road to a knowledge of the unconscious activities of the mind." Thus I asked myself the meaning, projected or not, of that first dream I had of flying back from Europe. Surely, I thought, it must have been important or I wouldn't have had it. And what was the meaning of that single mysterious phrase my seat companion spoke only minutes before the plane went down? He had just finished an article in the promotional airline magazine called "Remembering Franz: Kafka's Early Years," in which a variety of famous actors recreated mini-tableaux of the teenaged future Czech unhappy genius as he refused to eat a torte, stared at a large and furry brown dog, brooded in the back of his high school classroom from behind a sea of other pupils' hands. My companion, I remember, had closed the magazine, slipped it into the pouch in front of him, and stretched for a moment. Then, turning from me, he looked out the smudgy window, muttered the phrase, "embarrassingly high," and at once fell straight to sleep.

Clearly, the group of scantily clad Egyptological schoolgirls that followed was no more than an example of a dream-diversion, an image put there by the subconscious in order to distract the dreamer from the importance of the earlier message, and for a while it had worked, using as it did the triple attraction of sex, the afterlife, and a good education. Still, for a researcher as experienced as me, that phrase, "embarrassingly high," especially when spoken by a figure who was clearly meant to be my double (that is, we both occupied the same seat), who, although he had disguised this fact in my dream by pretending to have a life of his own, even supporting this by complaining about his job (a corporate psychologist) and showing me pictures of his family (a boy, a girl, a wife, a golden retriever), was child's play, or close to it.

The "embarrassing" part, of course, was easy enough to understand. The dictionary defined the word as "to be ashamed, to be found wanting, or caught at a loss, as, 'I am temporarily embarrassed for cash,'" so that the speaker in my dream was in fact speaking from the posture of farewell, as one who had already declared himself at the same time both the doctor, pronouncing over the body, and the body itself. "Good-bye," he was saying. "I'm embarrassed. So long."

Then, on the heels of that simple deduction, the meaning of the "high" portion of the phrase became apparent. The "high," of course, represented nothing more or less than the traditional concept of heaven—that place above the clouds where we go on living forever, that goal of mankind since time immemorial to somehow escape the pull of gravity, which even the American Indians recognized as ninety-five percent of the aging process, and so buried their dead on poles raised above the ground. Thus, the dream was saying, a part of me, my past, was already dead, while the other half, the present, would go on unsure, but full of hope.

As for Gigi, wherever she may be right now, chatting with some alter ego of mine or someone else's, I hope she's happy. Clearly we were meant to be together, but not for long. The one real surprise I had during our singular visit to Bill and Lib (in that city dedicated to the memory of a dead American rock-and-roll singing idol, his very name an ironic anagram of the word "lives," so that the graffiti sprayed along the walls of that sepulchral metropolis, "Elvis Lives," is in itself the two halves of our existence, this world and the next) had come over that last meal at the Chinese restaurant.

"Of course," Lib had told me as she masticated the remains of a sweet-and-sour hush puppy, "Gigi isn't Gigi's real name," but Madeline, which they'd chosen on the occasion she was conceived, during a drive-in movie, *Horror Night*, which included the Poe classic, "The Fall of the House of Usher."

But, Lib continued, when her daughter was young she was so restless, always in a such hurry to be somewhere ("Oh, Mom," Gigi had said), the kind of child who had barely finished a project before she began to move on to the next, that it didn't take them long to abandon that old first name of Madeline and change it, in the spirit of her own love of brevity, to just initials, which, Lib told me, "stand, as you surely must know by now, for Going, Gone."

KARMA

I

"It's like toppling down the stairs of one of those old-fashioned apartment buildings," Celia was saying in reply to one of my usual questions about the nature of an eternity of endless rebirth. "You know—five or six flights with flocked, faded, flowered paper on the walls, a little landing on each floor where you can slow down and focus for a second, take field notes if you want, but then you keep on falling."

"OK," I said, because Celia had made a study of those things ever since her mother had begun to support her daughter's way through art school by working as a psychic. She had specialized in finding missing people, and was good enough to be flown around the country courtesy of various police departments needing her services. "I see a red barn, and cows, and a bottle of eau de cologne," she'd say, and then fly home again. That is until shortly after Celia had gotten her degree, and the source of her mother's talent proved to be a malignant brain tumor.

All of this led, as you can well imagine, to countless discussions about the source of not only her mother's inspiration, but inspiration in general. It meant, Celia used to say, echoing Croce, that if art was merely a form of intuition, then her mother's visions of those frightening clues was also art. "Don't forget," she reminded me, "a few years before she died she woke up with a vision of a small flying pig accompanied by a muffled scream, and from this she was able to discover the decomposed body of Little Johnnie Tracinski in an abandoned pork butcher's where the child had apparently jumped from the rafters in his Superman cape, which had become wedged between a crossbeam, leaving him hanging there for the better part of a year. And what would your average museum make of that, Mr. Smarty?"

I had to admit I had no reply.

The object of my own art (did I mention that I was an artist?), rather than depending on the vagaries of intuition, chose to rest upon a single universal theme, one which I repeated in each of my installations: namely, out of discomfort and even pain, beauty rises. In my first show, for example, I had taken various dogs, cats, and even a large, white bunny from the local animal shelter and, in imitation of several large cosmetic firms, inflamed their mucous membranes, creating suppurating lesions and introducing multiple open sores so that they could be shown against a backdrop of beautiful high-fashion models (well, pictures of them actually, as most of the models I had asked refused to do it) whose beauty, even though great to begin with, clearly had been enhanced through the use of the products those animals had helped to develop.

My best-known piece thus far, called *Fetch*, involved the loss of one large dog each day of the show (it was up for a week) by hurling the unfortunate creature into a brick gallery wall at sixty miles per hour, next to a new (rented) Corvette so that patrons could see how (according to the people at General Motors) the crash tests using live animals helped contribute to the overall design and safety of the car. Because these shows were costly, however (*Fetch*, for example, had resulted in the gallery director being fired, to say nothing of the car rental), I had been trying to lower the scale of my work, say, down to a glass tank of cancer-filled rats which was to be placed in front of photos of cancer-free boys and girls in order to demonstrate how medical research was saving lives. The difficulty I was having was that by the time most of the rats had been sufficiently carcinified they tended to die, and although I could have replaced them with others, it seemed ethically important to begin and end the show with the same ones. At that moment, none were lasting more than four or five days.

Such, in addition to the increasing difficulty of simply finding a job that would pay the rent and buy enough rats to complete my art, were the problems I had before me. In fact, my position was a tricky one. My former employment, as an orderly at the State Hospital for the Criminally Insane, had been abruptly terminated just a few months earlier when, on my day off, an earthquake had leveled the entire building, killing everyone inside. As a result, I found myself caught between the prospect of finding some entirely new, less congenial line of work, or waiting a while for the numbers of the criminally insane to build back up again. (The bad news, I told myself, was losing all those maniacs at one fell swoop; it would take time before the courts, dogged as they were by delays and so on, could process enough to open a new institution. The good news, of course, was that all the other staff had been killed along with them, and so when a new institution did open, I'd be at the top of the list.) In the meantime I'd decided to buy myself time by initiating a series of smallish convenience store robberies—say, a couple a month—in order to meet expenses.

It was, I think, Wordsworth who one day found himself, in the midst of mourning his dead daughter, "surprised," as he put it, "by joy." So was I when, one morning about ten, I opened the door of my apartment to find myself being arrested for the robbery that I had committed just a few days earlier.

It had been late at night, and fortunately cold enough so the ski mask I was wearing didn't attract the attention it sometimes did, as I stood at the end of a line of teenagers waiting at the counter for change for their video games. An elderly gentleman in a burnoose sat reading a newspaper printed in some incomprehensible script and ignored the lot of us. When he at last looked up and the teenagers had all been grudgingly served, my time came. I unzipped from the pocket of my light-blue windbreaker the Operation Desert Storm Commemorative .45 auto, with its special inscription ("America Is # 1") and its sandblasted handle, and said in my calmest voice, "While I have no wish on earth to do you personal harm, unless you hand over the contents of the cash drawer immediately, I'll begin shooting."

Although my speech had its desired effect, luck, it seemed, was not to be on my side. Just as I was leaving, one of the teenagers, apparently surprised by the joy of winning a free game, leapt away from his machine, Menace to Society, and flailed his arms into a display of sour-cream-and-onion snack chips. The rack on which they were hung snagged the back of my ski mask in such a way that I could no longer see through the eyeholes, and I was forced to remove it to make my exit. I'd hoped, as anyone would, that perhaps the remote television camera might be turned off that evening in an effort to save electricity (I'd heard that was often the case), but as you may have guessed, I was not to be so fortunate.

The two policemen who came to arrest me, Gus and Jake, were surprisingly cordial, and became even more so when, as they waited for me to get dressed, they learned I had been a friend of Celia's mother, with whom they had worked on the case of Little Francine Hasley, a child who had disappeared from a crowded mall one day while shopping with her mother (a convicted klepto, by the way), and had turned up, through the help of psychic power, twenty years later working as a waitress on the day shift of a Howard Johnson's, living with an unemployed tennis pro named Raul. The only clue, the awestruck officers informed me, had been the three syllables: Ho, Jo, Pro.

I left a call on Celia's answering machine explaining what had happened and left for police headquarters with Jake and Gus, and there is no doubt in my mind we would have arrived had not the brakes of their police cruiser (regular maintenance being one of the victims of recent government cutbacks) failed on a critical turn just as we were at the edge of the Eastside

Reservoir, sending all three of us (thank God they hadn't bothered to use handcuffs) plunging straight into its murky depths, from which only I emerged. I stood at the edge and said a silent prayer for the drowned officers as I dripped on the discarded cans and disposable diapers that lined the banks. Then I fished two dimes from the soggy pockets of my trousers and, deciding to trust my future to the majesty of the law, called the station to tell them what had happened.

My public defender, it turned out, was also an artist, and, as "one of the last abstract expressionists" (this was his description) he explained how he at that moment in his career was forcing himself to work for the county judicial system in order to support his art. "At least in my work those poor dogs and cats don't suffer," he jeered at me, thus proving he'd missed the whole point. I reminded him about the toxic chemicals used to produce those gloomy pigments he seemed so fond of, and of the exploited workers who made the canvases on which he slopped his stuff. "And the product of all of this," I told him, "is something you call Beauty, but it's just that you are shutting your eyes to those parts you don't want to see."

"Huh," he grunted, and whether it was the result of his professional jealousy or the weight of the video testimony against me I'll never know, but in practically no time I found myself serving the maximum sentence permitted under the law.

Prison was pretty much what anyone would imagine: sterile, overcrowded, full of poor food and accompanied by plenty of body odor, but offering lots of free time and a fair library (though leaning toward Ayn Rand). Many of my fellow prisoners, it turned out, were artists as well, and spent their hours drawing their memories of home or personal criminal highlights on cheap white handkerchiefs which commanded surprisingly high prices at the prison gift shop. They were so much in demand, in fact, that some of the men had learned to turn out five or six of these heartrending sketches an hour. With each selling at from twenty to fifty dollars, even minus the gift shop's markup, several of my fellow inmates were making far more from their art than they ever had when free, knowing, of course, that the minute they ceased to be incarcerated the prices of any new non-penitentiary-based work they might produce would drop back again to near zero. It seemed that people outside of prison simply weren't interested in scenes of people standing in an unemployment line, sitting at a desk across from a parole officer, or waiting for a bus.

My cell mates, Martin and Shorty and Bo and Cyril and Rasheed, were all basically decent human beings gone wrong, and, except for Cyril, who whenever the cafeteria served Sloppy Joes was driven to prolonged and unaccountable depressions, we all got along well enough, and made it a habit to hold regular "gripe sessions," as well as discussion groups on political or philosophical issues.

Curiously, it was at one of these later sessions, one of our "'What Is Art?' Saturdays," that real change finally came about. It all began when I expressed the opinion you're already familiar with, that art is something good that comes from something bad. Bo disagreed, and quoted Oscar Wilde to the effect that the only reason the lower classes commit crimes is because they are incapable of the superior stimulation the rich derive from art.

"No!" shouted Martin, who declared the purpose of art was to let us see the world in a new light, to make things new, but no sooner had he expressed this thought than he was interrupted by Cyril, who simultaneously agreeing and disagreeing, remarked that while the results of both art and crime were to redistribute wealth, art also aimed for a return to the primal order of peace and stillness, or better yet, to stop time entirely. Cyril was doing ten to fifteen for shooting his brother in the head with a shotgun, and oddly enough, his defense at his trial was similar: that he was only trying to wipe the smile off his victim's face. Rasheed, a Marxist, simply declared that art was an illusion created solely for the oppression of the working class, its end product being a whole new series of useless items the working class couldn't afford to buy, thus another reminder of its inferiority. To that degree, he said, he agreed with Bo. Shorty claimed it was a male substitute for giving birth, and while no one particularly agreed with him, his words carried some authority because before his imprisonment for forgery he had been one of the few artists of any of us who actually had made a living at it.

"Wait a minute," Cyril said. "Are you saying art is the essence of life or just an escape from it?"

"Who cares?" said Rasheed. "But speaking of escape, isn't it time we began thinking a little along those lines?"

So we began, as a group, to move the discussion from the philosophical to the practical, from thought, as they say, to action. Bo, for example, offered to explore digging a tunnel, and cited as his credentials his past experience as a plumber's helper. Shorty declared tunnels to be passé. "A cliché," he said, "out of every prison movie ever made. Do you realize how few actual successful escapes have ever been made through tunnels?" Cyril added that what he thought we really needed was one good laundry truck so we could get out disguised as bags of socks and dirty underwear.

Finally, at the close of our brainstorming session, we had a plan. First we decided (borrowing a concept from Edward Kienholz) we would create a series of lifelike statues based on ourselves, made out of leftover bread. We would leave them scattered around the cell in postures that would make it appear as if we hadn't left the cell at all, but instead had become permanently frozen. Next, because our location on the top floor virtually ruled out tunnels anyway, we would climb out onto the roof by means of the ventilating system, and then, under the diversion of a total solar eclipse due in about a month, it would be simple to throw down a rope, lower ourselves into a truck, and, with most of us disguised as prisoners' laundry, for Rasheed, wearing the gravy-stained uniform of a guard, to drive us to freedom.

Needless to say, it worked.

II

In J. M. W. Turner's great painting, *The Burning of the Houses of Lords and Commons, October 16, 1834*, one can not only see at its center the red plume of flame rising to the sky, but that same flame distorted and doubled in the water beneath it. There is also a bridge and some boats, and a bit of shore as well, but the key part is still the fire, that burning in the distance which leaves us, the viewers, moved but also safe. And isn't that what art's about—this consuming without being consumed, this watching of heat without the danger of being burned; to commit a crime, be caught, go to jail, and then escape without ever having to leave one's favorite cozy chair?

Celia's own art had consisted of first coating herself and her clothing with a flame-retarding chemical, then, with a nearby water-filled wading pool of sufficient size to douse the flames, to set herself on fire and videotape the results. The first few times, understandably, were essentially just a run of the fifteen to twenty or so feet from the point of ignition to the wading pool, but as Celia went on she grew bolder. Later versions included the completion of various tasks—threading a needle, building a low wall out of bricks, typing a letter to a celebrity, and so on—before she allowed herself to make the dive to the pool. Later, the artifacts of her deed—the scorched letter, the poorly constructed wall, the needle and charred thread—were sold as a permanent reminder of the art itself: the fire and simultaneous act of creation.

"Dangerous?" Celia had said. "Well, yes, but my art is about things to do and time to do them in, and not at all about safety or about danger." And in fact most of her performances went off flawlessly except for a few earlier ones where, she said, when it came to applying the chemical retardant, she was in just too big a hurry. "These scars," she added, "are my karma."

My own karma had caused me, at about the age of eight, to be one of those very missing persons who a few years later Celia's mother would become famous for discovering, although in my case, whether it was because there were no such talented psychics around, or because my real parents, after the first few grainy reproductions on milk cartons and bus posters (I never did photograph well), just gave up and found other interests, I never knew.

My own story began one day when I was walking home from school in the third grade and a large car pulled up next to me. Someone inside said, "Hey, kid, get in." Because I wasn't paying much attention (I assumed the voice belonged to some neighbor my parents had sent to fetch me—maybe there'd been an accident or something), I complied without looking, and it was only twenty or thirty minutes into the ride, when the driver handed me a handkerchief that had been soaked in ether and instructed me to "breathe deeply," that I suspected something was wrong.

I breathed in, and when I woke I was in a large bed full of stuffed animals and with a bedspread that featured a cowboy roping a lone steer. A man and woman were standing over me, and in a few minutes, when the effects of the drug had worn off, I heard the woman speak.

"My name is Thea Montgomery," she said, "and this is my husband, Lance. Several months ago we lost our own son, Little Bobby, and last week, after trying everything to bring him back, we decided to give up hope and instructed Martin, our chauffeur, to be on the alert for a likely replacement. Perhaps this was too important a responsibility to be given to a man whose failing eyesight and bad judgment have become a real cause for concern over these past years, but we had no one else to trust, and have decided to accept his choice of you, whatever else might be said about it, simply as our karma. This is your new home, where you will be raised in the finest surroundings, the most up-to-date decor, and the most love Lance and I can offer, keeping in mind, of course, that you are not Little Bobby." Thea wiped a tear from her eye. "What is your name?" she asked.

"Whatever you'd like," I replied, and from that moment I began my new life.

III

In J. M. W. Turner's masterpiece of the nineteenth century, *The Burning of the Houses of Lords and Commons, October 16, 1834,* even the most callous viewer cannot fail to salute the awesome beauty that is the direct result of that terrible fire. So it was with mixed emotions that I viewed the videotape of Celia's last, now legendary performance, in which, after setting herself on fire, she dialed the toll-free number of the customer complaint line provided by her low-cost health care provider, and waited to a musical background of "Raindrops Keep Falling on My Head" as she was kept on hold. Even on tape, one cannot look at the artifacts of those astounding seventeen minutes—the half-melted receiver and the plastic circle of what turned out to be a very leaky wading pool with its urgent calligraph of charcoal smears and smudges, and not be moved.

Turning off the video monitor, I found myself remembering, to my surprise, a poem I'd read on the very last day of my own third grade class before I went to live with Lance and Thea. It began, "I am the North Wind, and spare nothing beneath my wintry blast," and was accompanied by a drawing of an old man with puffed cheeks and icicles in his beard. "What lasts?" I asked myself, and thought of Celia, her mother, Jake and Gus, all the patients and staff at what used to be the State Hospital, even my former cell mates, Bo and Shorty and Rasheed and Cyril and Martin, who, I had read in the papers, had been recaptured, one by one.

And what had it meant that one day before Celia's mom lifted the veil that divides this world and the next forever, suddenly, from somewhere in the midst of incomprehensible ravings, she had turned to her daughter and spoken in a voice filled with utter calm and authority, the voice almost of a completely different woman, the simple phrase, "See you soon"? Had she known at that moment the terrible fate that awaited her daughter? And what, from the perspective of eternity, was "soon"? Five years? Ten? A hundred? Then she returned to "test patterns," as Celia described her mother's ravings: descriptions of a car with huge tail fins, a cage of chickens, darkness, a puddle of water, and a round ashtray with the marks of several stubbed-out cigarettes smeared across its bottom.

Did life, I asked myself, simply flow from life, like a river from a lake, or was there some greater purpose? And if there was none, then did life arrive all by itself? Did it flow from the nothingness that was here before us? Those were, and still are, big questions, and I'm not sure of any answers. All things fall and rise again. "The wind goeth toward the south and turneth about unto the north," saith the Preacher, "it whirleth continually." So why then, out of all those four winds, is it only the north one I remember? Does pointing to any part of anything infer the presence of the rest? Is to know the north to imply the other three? Does to have a child imply the child's absence, and likewise, does having a missing child imply the possibility of return some day in the future, his features thickened, the lines of pain now visible around his eyes, the lines of disappointment beginning to cluster near his mouth, his limp, his ever-more stooped back, the tremble of his hand, all these as inescapable as if that child had stayed at home, had been tucked in each night by caring parents, had grown and worked and been in love. And in the end, both lives, the one lived and the one unlived, "They whirleth."

"See you soon," Celia's mom had said, but who knows what she meant by "see"? Had she meant it in the same sense as those psychic clues that used to slide beneath the curtain of her eyes, somehow enhanced by the gentle pressure of the tumor in her head? Or maybe she just meant "see" in an everyday sense, as "what is seen." But what do we see? Is it what is there or what we think is there? And of all the millions of connections between one part of the world and all the rest, one minute and all others, how many are we capable of recording before our brain cells at last grow tired, lie down, call it a day, give up, take a rest and just plain sleep?

ANOTHER LIFE

I. Tibor

The first thing is, everyone died.

II. Little Man

There I was, wiping up the rich broth left from my bowl of greasy stew with a ragged piece of bread as if I hadn't eaten in a week, when in fact it had just been since early morning. "What's your name?" the woman asked me. She was tall and blond, and wearing shiny pink lipstick, a strange thing, I thought, considering that the cabin we were in was situated in such a remote part of the woods. Her lipstick was a little smeared in one corner, something I had always found attractive. Of course, just exactly where the cabin was in relation to the woods as a whole I had absolutely no idea. I had simply started out, earlier that day, amid the towering trees, grasping brambles and spore-laden fingers of ferns, following first one path then another, until I finally became so entangled that even if I'd known what direction to go in, I couldn't possibly have found it.

And yes, I had encountered the traditional friendly animals: bluebirds swooping overhead to lead me onward, the beckoning trumpet of the majestic elk, squirrels chattering their instructions through the branches, wolves on distant ridges assuming the improbable poses of bird dogs, muzzles pointing. The only problem was, as helpful as they all undoubtedly meant to be, each pointed in a different direction, guiding me not to any sheltered habitation, but all flying, leaping, and calling out for me to notice various sites of recent environmental degradation, no doubt trying in their

129

pathetic animal fashion to communicate to me and all mankind that their species were well on their way to extinction solely due to the arrogance of me and other humans.

Then, all at once, there was the cabin. It was practically invisible amid the opaque greenery, and I had nearly reached its door when I looked down from all the gesticulating wildlife to realize I had been following a faint trail all along. The logs the cabin had been built from were overgrown with moss, and its windows were so covered with vines that my first impression was not of a cabin, but simply an entrance straight into the foliage itself. And then behind it, as in a fairy tale, the woman had been standing, her hair swept back in two long blond braids, tied at the ends by two dark, bloody ribbons.

Without saying a word she motioned me to sit down at her table. Wiping her hands on her apron (a coarse white material, which looked homemade), she took down a rough wooden bowl from the shelf, walked to the bubbling pot of stew in the fireplace and filled the bowl. Then she placed it before me on the table with a golden loaf of bread, warm from the oven. It was only after I had completed this impromptu dinner, accompanied by a small glass of *vin ordinaire*, and was swabbing up the last of the meal with a crust of bread, that she finally spoke. "Have you a name?" she inquired.

"Well then," she said, noticing I was at a loss for words, "I'll just call you Little Man, in honor of a son I had, a talented musician and perhaps even a prodigy, who, at the age of four, while beating out the timpani section of the "Ode to Joy" on his practice drum set, caught one of the tips of the sticks in his tiny mouth and choked to death. It's not the kind of thing a mother gets over very easily."

I looked around. The furnishings of the cabin's interior were conventional—perhaps suspiciously so. I was seated in a rustic chair at a rustic table. There were rustic shelves and cabinets, a television covered with bark, a folding sofa bed, and a few dozen jars, all filled with bright liquids. Attached to each piece of furniture was a sign, clearly denoting its name and pronunciation, both in English and French, followed by a date that I supposed was the year of manufacture.

Weary from my repeated attempts to remember one name from my past with which I could replace the unfortunate appellation "Little Man," I fell asleep, waking only later, in the near middle of the night, to find myself engaged, along with my mysterious hostess, in such classic and modern acts of sexual congress as The Polar Bear, The Suspension Bridge, The Shoemaker and the Elves, Crop Rotation, The Spinning Wheel, The Bumblebee's Adventure, The Interrupted Lesson, The Smoking Gun, The Grassy Knoll, The Petrified Forest, The First Amendment, The Unanswered Question, The Star, The Easter Basket, and A Day on the Farm (a variation of Crop Rotation).

The next morning I awoke curiously refreshed. The mysterious woman (who looked, in case you are wondering, nothing like my mother, who was more a short, swarthy, asymmetrical version of Natalie Wood) had set out a breakfast of English muffins, a cheese omelet, fresh juice, coffee, and a vitamin tablet, all of which I consumed with pleasure. When I had finished she hurried me over the threshold of her cabin. "Don't be late for work, Little Man," she said. Then she kissed my cheek and slammed the door behind me.

Who was it who said that long voyages can often lose themselves in travel? There I was, just starting out, without the least clue as to my destination and saddled with a name that might belong to a racing pigeon, and already I was late. Would I ever find where I was headed? What, I wondered, was my job?

The forest seemed to have changed in my nightlong absence. The formerly friendly, perhaps even presumptuous animals of the previous day had vanished, leaving behind stones, bark, fallen leaves and trampled limbs. The air had grown cold and the trails of yesterday seemed even more invisible, overgrown and impenetrable. The grey morning wore on. I walked for miles. Somewhere, on a random rock,

I left behind the genuine leather briefcase my benefactress had provided me for my day at work. About noon a light drizzle began to fall. I held the *Wall Street Journal* she had given me at breakfast over my head until it became soggy and useless. Settling myself beneath a stately oak, I took a few minutes to stitch myself a cap of leaves, and continued on my way.

The rain persisted, increasing in its intensity with every hour. I soon gave up all efforts to discover where I was employed (surely I was terminally late for work in any case), and decided to seek higher ground. I climbed that day, and the next, and the next, and the whole time the rain continued. Finally, near the top of a peak, I found an abandoned cave, the entrance of which had apparently been used as a storage facility by mountain climbers, for there were several cases of canned beans and a box of granola bars, all quite edible. I decided to wait out the rain, and so I sat, like a pathetic, denuded bear in the mouth of its den, eating oatmeal, nuts and beans, watching the water level rise in the valley beneath me.

The rain continued. Days, maybe even weeks passed without a change, except in its intensity, so that every so often there would be a fine mist and it appeared the rain was ending, then the downpour would resume. As I looked out I could see the valley slowly disappear into a vast, tumultuous lake, and still the rain kept coming. At first, it seemed a blessing in a way, for as the water rose, the mountain top I occupied filled with animals trying to escape death by drowning— exhausted deer, panting chipmunks, weary raccoons, and drenched opossums—and I took advantage of their weakened condition to supplement my diet with fresh-cooked meat (I had a disposable butane lighter with me, so starting a fire was no problem). I would sleep, eat, huddle near the fire, trying to keep off the growing damp, then venture out into the rain to bludgeon some new shivering creature who had approached my cave in search of shelter.

The rain continued. Soon I no longer even had to leave the entrance of the cave to find my prey, as my home filled with small shivering bodies. I killed them, skinned them, ate them, and still they came, more frightened of the rising waters than of death.

The water had risen nearly to the cave's mouth when I decided I could no longer take the endless waiting. I refused to be just another victimized bunny or disheartened wolverine. Clearly (for I had explored the mountain above me and there was no shelter on higher ground) I had no choice. I removed my shoes, a sturdy pair of oxblood wing-tips, and my grey striped trousers. Then, after loosening my tie and covering the tops of more than four hundred empty bean cans with the skins of small dead animals, I made a kind of pontoon raft and pushed off into the murky water.

For a surprisingly long time, considering the nature of the materials from which my craft was built, my little boat endured. Then, one by one, like the tops of bongo drums left out beneath the force of a hurricane on a formerly festive tropical isle, the skins covering the cans began to work their way loose, and the cans themselves began to fill with water. These I cut away until bit by bit my raft grew smaller, and at the very end it was reduced to two cans, one for each hand. Then they too began to fill. I could no longer see my mountain or the cave, nor could I steer amid the aimless tide. I floated, helpless as in a dream, growing colder, and more numb. At last I began to feel a slow luxurious seeping warmth which traveled from my fingers and toes up to my legs, arms and torso, until mercifully, eventually, finally, everything was just about to turn completely dark.

The ark was very large.

III. Ooglik

Despite everything that's happened to me since, I still remember that terrible day when my parents, two decent people who I'm sure, under different circumstances, would have laid down their lives for me, called me aside to explain what they had planned.

"Son," my mother said, "we're very fond of you, but now that you're nearly grown, it's time you knew just how bad things really are." She smoothed her brows with one short, ivory-colored finger. It was characteristic of my mother that even during moments of high emotion, her makeup and composure remained perfect. "As you know, we have been starving for nearly a year, and though it's true that occasionally your father manages to trap a ptarmigan, or, after waiting hours by a breathing hole, harpoons a seal, these instances are exceptions rather than the rule. The fact is, there simply is not enough food to go around, and one of us must go. Now, who shall it be? Let's think it through: It can't be your father, because, bad as things already are, he is the only one who is, under happier circumstances, capable of catching food on a regular basis. That leaves you and me, a hard choice for any mother. But consider: If I were to sacrifice myself and then you were to somehow die, our genetic line would be extinct. If, on the other hand, you left home, and died while I stayed alive, as depressed as I might be after learning of your fate, I still would be able to replicate a variant of yourself—not yourself exactly, but a little posthumous sister or brother who would be more of a genetic match than your own children."

Mom wiped a tear, or something, from her eye and picked up a tissue to blot the pathetic swatch of blood-and-blubber lipstick she had applied earlier to keep our family's spirits up. I had to admit her reasoning was impeccable. "Good-bye," I said, as Father stood by the door holding it open so as not to prolong the emotionality of the moment. Mother, on the other hand, hid her feelings by rearranging their meager piles of ration from three stacks to two. Then I stepped out into the Arctic night.

"Be strong," I told myself. In only two more months it would be daybreak, and the herds of caribou and schools of salmon would be on the move again. Who was to decide my lot was necessarily the wrong one? Only time would tell if being the person on the outside was bad or good. I slung the bag made out of an entire hollowed-out snowshoe hare (its mouth the opening and its rectum sewed shut) over my shoulder, and moved bravely toward my future.

Time passed and my initial resolve faded. Soon I found myself listening to the siren calls of drifts of snow and coverlets of ice to come, lie down, and sleep a while. Yet I knew that if I did, I would never rise again. I pulled my parka tightly around me and marched on. Suddenly, just a few yards to my right, I saw what was either an hallucination or salvation. An ungainly black and white flightless bird (evidently a survivor of an unsuccessful experiment to transplant a colony of these Antarctic avians, the precursors of an ill-fated theme park where visitors were expected to experience, in specially designed rides, the disasters of one failed polar expedition after another: crashed balloons, vicious huskies, frozen ponies, and even refreshment stands which, when arrived at through great peril, would be empty and useless) waddled toward me on webbed feet. How ironic, I thought, that this symbol of so many shipwrecked investment hopes should be the source of my possibly temporary salvation.

The bird (for it was no hallucination) waddled up to me, its vestigial wings outstretched as if about to greet some old friend, and who knows, perhaps it *had* bonded, as birds are prone to do, with one of those earlier entrepreneurs who had brought it here, and had been wandering the Arctic wastes ever since, calling into the darkness after its missing friend. But alas for it, I was not the one for whom it had been waiting. I took my knife and, embracing the child-size bird so that it could not break loose in its death struggles, plunged my blade into its heart. My first thrust, unhappily, was not fatal. The bird, formerly so elated to make my acquaintance, screamed and tried to pull away, its tiny wings pushing hard against my chest, its feet grasping for a foothold on the slippery slope, and its powerful beak rending the air over one of my shoulders. I knocked it down, afraid it would escape, stabbed it again and again, and with every blow it convulsed and filled the empty air with cries for help. Then, at last, it died.

I made a cap out of its skin, and after eating the first real nourishment I'd had in weeks, packed the remainder of its flesh in freezer bags, and once again began my desperate journey, never sure where I was headed or why, but moving onward nonetheless. More time passed. I had long ago eaten the last of my extroverted prey when one morning I awoke to a sound which makes the blood of all of those who live here in the Arctic, human and animal alike, clot with the hormones of fear and dread. It was the first sharp crack that signaled the beginning of the breakup of the ice pack. Additional cracks soon followed as I watched with paralyzed fascination my domain becoming smaller, and then smaller yet with each crack, until finally my escape route—if ever there was one—to the shore disappeared. My icy homestead subdivided from an acre to half that size, and then to half again, and so on, until at last I was adrift on a piece of ice no larger than a living room rug I once saw advertised on a page of the *National Geographic*, next to an article, "The Amazing Arctic," which featured my uncle.

Deep in the slate-grey waters that surrounded my shrinking chunk of ice I could see the giant prowling shapes of killer whales. My end, I reflected, would be swift and bloody. I took a deep breath and prepared for the worst. To my surprise, for the first time since my departure from home the air was not its customary crisp, unscented, pristine self. Instead, cold as it was, it was ripe with the droppings of what seemed to be many animals—at least two, I thought, of every kind.

IV. Little Man

What good is a love song if everyone swoons to it? What good is a meal if everyone digests it at the same time? What good are these few precious days if I share them with you, whoever you are and whoever I am, two travelers, voyagers, just a couple of Odysseuses, interrupted by an island here, a shipwreck there, enchantresses and monsters, but always our journeys prevailing, losing one by one each comfort, until at last we're back home, our wives' tapestries finished, our houses full of petrified memories we weren't around to witness—the photos of the kids, the drawers full of t-shirts saying "Damn, I'm good!," the vacation brochures, the snapshots from parties, blurred, with the guests looking slightly too happy, the endless rounds of hugs, and always afterwards our heads suspended above, not quite touching, our pillows, our horses half-saddled outside in their stables, our cars resting above their grease pits, their drain plugs loosened but never quite removed, almost, nearly, just about, waiting, and if not for a birth, then for what?

I hung up the cap I'd stitched from leaves (which had held up surprisingly well) and looked around. There were a few chickens, a rooster, a pair of ducks quacking in their pen, a donkey and its mate, two brown dogs, a cat, two parakeets (Pretty Girl and Pretty Boy), and that was about it. As soon as I was settled I inquired about the lions, the elephants, the scorpions, the snakes, for starters, and got a "What, are you crazy?" look in reply.

"Take a whiff," my host said. "I can't keep up with this bunch. Why would you want any more?"

He had a point. His present acute depression, he told me, was the result of having, despite his better judgment, believed he had been chosen for a divine mission, and so he had built a boat, collected a few animals, stockpiled provisions, and then put out to sea. Now he was in the exact opposite position of all those cold war survivalists after the breakup of the former Soviet Union with their fallout shelters, camo gear and Russian dictionaries. It had been raining, all right, but it was scarcely a Flood, capital F.

"What about your family?" I asked him.

"At home," he said. "They thought I was crazy, and the neighbors agreed. My wife made me sign everything over to her before I left, and I thought, sure, OK, it's the end of the world; why shouldn't she have the Barry Manilow records? But it turned out the whole time she was seeing the guy who had fixed our garbage disposal once, so now all I have to my name is this ridiculous boat." He rested his head in two large hands. "Eggs," he said.

"What?" I answered.

"I hope you like eggs."

As a matter of fact, I hated eggs, and it all began when I was a child. Back then, in one of the few memories I still possess, I had been given away by my literati parents to a band of gypsies in return for having the dents taken out of their car, and also in the hope I would be spared the ruthless advance of neonaturalism across the land.

"Who are your characters?" the neonaturalists would demand. "Where do they live? Tell me their emotions. What are they wearing?" And all across the land their interrogatees such as myself would tremble in fear.

"Use the five senses," these arbiters of so-called style would hiss at the pupils in Ms. Zachman's third grade creative writing class, and at me in particular. "Show and don't tell," they would say, shaking their bony fingers in my direction, their coarse grey clothing smelling faintly of pine cleaner and pepperoni pizza, their favorite lunch. Afterwards, those children foolish enough to "tell" were taken away—to be trained, they said, to observe small details—but wherever they went, they were never seen again.

"It's too late for your mom and me," my father, a neo-surrealist, whispered to me one evening, "but if you can get away, you might have a chance."

"Yes," my mother added, strands of her sooty hair stuck to her cheeks like cracks in a plate the shape of a human face issued by the Franklin Mint, guaranteed to appreciate in value or your money back. "Speaking as an old-fashioned neopost-modernist, our luck has just about run out."

So I bade farewell to my parents forever, and was handed over to an old woman in the gypsies' summer camp near an intersection famous for accidents. She looked me over. "You," she snorted. "You're too skinny to pull out dents and stuff them with Bondo the way most of our menfolk do. I'll put you in charge of the chickens."

Thus it became my job to feed, protect, disinfect, make comfortable, and most important, guard these feathered engines of ovum from the predations of the night. At the start I had no strong feelings one way or the other about chickens. The nights of early fall were balmy, and I slept on a canvas cot near the entrance to the coop, my head near its open door, my feet pointing to the back wall. But fall soon turned to winter. Snow collected on the roof of the coop; the nights grew increasingly bitter, and I was forced to move inside. At first the birds huddled together for warmth, needing only their own kind to derive a necessary level of comfort. Then, as the cold increased, first one, then another of the frost-fearing avians came to perch on my legs, my chest, my arms, and other parts of my body in search of warmth. I admit that in the beginning the sensation of being sat upon by twenty or thirty pounds of fowl was pleasant, in a way, like lying beneath a wheezing quilt of down, and even though it has always been my habit to sleep with my mouth open, I was never more inconvenienced than occasionally having to remove a scaly foot, or to dislodge a loose feather that had floated midway into my throat.

Then, one night, I had the strangest dream. I was a fish, and swimming (what else?) through the water in search of food. I peeked into brilliant coral reefs and combed sandy bottoms, poked through waving beds of kelp, all to no avail, when at last I saw my prey: a small blue and gold creature who was also swimming in search of food. As quietly as I could I swam up behind it and seized it in my teeth. But just then my prey seized a smaller fish between its teeth, and the smaller one seized a yet smaller one and so on, until, as in the reverse of an old cartoon, suddenly instead of the single meal I had intended, I had an infinite number, but I was no more full than when I seized my very first victim. I awoke, groggy. I tried to suck in air and nothing came, I coughed and no air was expelled. I thought I was going to die.

I realized what must have happened. A single egg, hot and steaming from the body of a hen perched exactly over my face, must have been deposited directly into my open mouth and throat. I reached in with the index finger of my right hand and tried to push it down, but it wouldn't budge. I tried to pull it up, to break it, but couldn't. Desperately, wildly, I looked around for something to remove the obstruction, but all I could see was a pile of soft, sleeping hens, and still I could not breathe! I stumbled out of the henhouse and looked crazily around at the snow-covered ground for a knife or fork. Nothing. Then all at once I had an idea, a chance in a thousand. Chokingly, impossibly I climbed the icy rungs of the ladder leading to the roof of the coop and, with only moments to live, positioned myself over a four-foot mound of frozen chicken droppings the gypsies were saving to put in their garden when spring came. I staggered to the edge of the roof and then dropped straight onto the icy pyramid, aiming the force of the blow at my diaphragm. Needless to say, it was this primitive Heimlich maneuver which, in the end, expelled the deadly object from my throat.

And though since then I have had no aversion to the meat of chicken, or indeed any fowl, I have been unable to touch, taste, smell, or even gaze upon those repulsively cold (when refrigerated) and warm (when not) oval bombs of white and yellow, those saucer-size handouts in which a future fetus rests, those tiny ergometric waiting rooms which, when fertile, conceal a still-shut eye or half-formed wing or beak submerged, like an idea not fully realized inside a yolky dream, but which, on the other hand, if not fertile, are even worse: the mindless yellow zero of pure potential, empty of all specific sums, a mockery of the source of our own existence— mere eggs—slippery when fried, rubbery when boiled, when poached the consistency of a brain without a single memory to dignify its brief existence; the pure terror of all that is without a point, the pathos of the seed fallen on barren ground, the thought never expressed, the love never declared, in short, our lives and everything that's in them.

Days on board the ark passed with tedium. Although I was gratified to have been rescued, and tried to make myself as useful as possible, it was clear that my host was a mentally disturbed individual, one who still regularly heard voices demanding he perform a whole series of tasks, and while some seemed useful ("Pick up the narrator"), and others nearly impossible ("Obtain a Ph.D. in particle physics"), it became clear, in effect, that my rescue had been, rather than any divine intervention, merely a matter of statistical probability. That is, if at any given moment there are X numbers of humans hearing Y numbers of instructions, eventually Z of those instructions are going to turn out to be useful. In other words, for every guy who builds a boat, most won't finish, but of those who do, for most it won't rain at all. Then, for a few others it will shower, and for still fewer, storm, until during an actual flood there may only be two or three guys in arks paddling around, and even then chances are they aren't really needed.

The sun had come out, but without maps or charts my host seemed content to simply drift. The only indications of our position I could detect were a slight shift in the placement of the stars and the fact that the weather was growing colder. Snow began to fall on an almost daily basis, and our visibility was reduced to nearly zero. The nights, now that I could no longer bring myself to take advantage of a warm chicken, were cold, and as ungrateful as it may sound, I wished I were elsewhere.

At last, late one afternoon (though it was hard to tell, because somehow we'd lost all daylight), I heard a thump and what sounded like a yell. I scrambled to the deck. There in the dark, through the falling snow, unnoticed by my captain, far below where I was standing, perched on top of a shrinking piece of ice, I could just barely discern the figure of a fur-clad Eskimo.

V. Ooglik

After my timely rescue from a disintegrating ice flow by a highly delusional amateur yachtsman and his mysterious passenger, I was in no position to be critical. Once on board, handicapped by language difficulties as I was, I mostly sat around restoring my strength with hard-boiled eggs and crusts of not-very-good dry bread until at long last our boat ran aground near Holland and we were towed into Amsterdam by the Dutch Navy.

Once on land, I made my way straight to a youth hostel, where I met Donna, an English major traveling through Europe for her junior year at Sarah Lawrence, who explained to me the principles of The Suspension Bridge, The Dangling Participle, and The Misplaced Modifier, and before I could protest she had twisted the syllables of my proud indigenous name into a sound very like the gasp of a dying penguin.

To summarize: Donna and I traveled together throughout Europe; I learned English; she took me back with her to her dorm where I became a momentary campus sensation, earning extra money by posing for life drawing classes. Then one day, conceptual art arrived and I was out of a job. I took to a life of crime—first robbing one-man photo booths, then mom-and-pop establishments, then family grocery stores, then paternalistic giant corporations. Eventually I began to deal in drugs, and it was in regard to one such transaction that I was sent to France where I was to pick up a shipment of drugs from a colorful group of Romanian gypsies and their tame bear, and then return with the drugs to the United States, where they would be funneled to a chain of yogurt parlors which also served as narcotics distribution centers. Little did I know that, following a gun battle that came as the result of the gypsies refusing to turn over the drugs, most of them would be killed, and my final destination would be none other than that most classic locale in all of prison literature, Devil's Island.

Whatever else may be said, certainly I can't deny that one of the odd benefits of my residence on The Island, as it was called by its residents, was an inordinate amount of time to ponder. Who, for one, was telling this, my story? And for another, if it was me, then how was it possible to be asking this question?

To take the easiest first: I was telling a story that I perceived to be mine, but which, I realized, could as easily be told by any number of other narrators. As to the second question, that of how I can be sure this was being told, I simply riposte that my asking the question at all was the answer.

While life there was no picnic, it is also true that the French, in the manner for which they are famous the world over, prepared even prison fare with *un certain style*. Even regarding items normally associated with *cuisine de prison*— bread and water, for example—I noticed that the baguettes were crusty and fresh baked each day, and the water had been shipped in from a renowned mineral spring outside Nantes. Likewise, our weekly ration of slop, as I called it, would arrive punctually every Wednesday seasoned with *herbes de provence* and sprinkled with *sauce normande*.

So in a way, my days were tolerable. My work assignment, unlike that of my fellow inmates, who worked in the cane fields, took into account my artistic background, and it became my job to create paintings of prisoners staring out to sea *(Thoughts of Home)*, standing surrounded by heaps of fallen chains *(Free at Last)*, men being whipped *(Ouch!)*, or under guard, working in the fields *(Wages of Sin)*. These I would turn out at the rate of about four each day, in different styles and mediums, and signed with different names. Then they would be sent to Paris, where they were sold by the prison's own gallery, Galerie d'Art Pathétique, and the profits returned to the state.

So went my days. Nights, however, were a different story. It was then my warder, the sadistic Maurice, would torment me with his endless playing of Edith Piaf records on a small portable record player, much as American teenagers used to possess in the 1950s. In the beginning, I confess, the effect was somewhat pleasurable, and for the first several months I actually looked forward to my nightly concert of "The Little Sparrow," as Maurice affectionately referred to her. It was only much later, in fact after a whole year had passed, that I began to understand the true cruelty of my captor. If I had to hear Maurice cackle in his badly accented English, "Lissen to ziz, you Eskimo," followed by "La Vie en rose," one more time I would hang myself. My guards, however, had long since removed all implements that might make such a violent act possible. Curiously, my paintings (and perhaps this was the real motivation behind my torture), driven as they were by nightly injections of new despair, became more and more in demand and brought in increasingly more revenue. Thus I became an even more valuable asset to the prison officials.

No, since taking my life was out of the question, there remained only one other possibility—escape. But having gotten from point A to point B, then to C, D and E, so to speak, could I ever retrace my steps, complex as they seemed, back home to A once again? Only time would provide an answer.

VI. Little Man

Midway through life's journey two roads diverged into a trackless wood, and I took both of them, which has made all the difference. The ark, as I called it, eventually ran aground, and I found myself in Amsterdam, home of chocolate, wooden shoes, and the world's most sensible policemen. The authorities, after impounding my host's animal cargo (which were looking fairly ill by then), put him "under observation" to assess the state of his mental health. My fellow passenger and I were allowed to leave, and so we did, he heading toward the student quarter and me wandering the streets lost, unsteady after all those days at sea, and dazed, in search of someone or something that would give me a direction to follow.

All at once I looked up from where I was standing in the street. There in a window was what appeared to be a re-creation of a rustic cabin, complete with log walls and hand-hewn furniture. A woman in a homespun dress sat knitting industriously, an inspiring contrast to what, as I looked around, were other women in other windows, each representing a particular historical period. No matter what era they were supposed to re-create, however, they were all watching on identical miniature televisions *Stand Up and Walk*, an audience-participation show dedicated to unfortunates of every stripe whose prize would be a vacation at some disreputable resort struggling vainly to increase its business by means of these giveaways. I smiled at this woman who had made herself an exception to an odious rule to indicate I admired her sense of industry. To my surprise she pushed the blond hair away from her face and signaled that I should come on up and visit.

Her name, it turned out, was Marnie, and her room was even smaller than it had appeared from the window. There was a couch carved from pine, with cushions filled with boughs and lumpy pine cones, a hastily built table, a mattress, and a tiny bath with a wash basin and a bidet disguised as a well. In one corner was a small refrigerator stocked with beer and soft drinks. "You look kind of dazed," she said. "Do you have any money?"

I reached in my jeans and pulled out a couple of soggy bills, having no idea how they got there. "Only these," I answered.

"Well," said Marnie, "that's a start. Lie down. I'll take care of you and then we'll talk for a while."

To summarize: Marnie nursed me back to health, at least enough to appear on *Stand Up and Walk*, where I won a trip to a down-scale resort in Romania. There I met a group of drug-running gypsies who were having language difficulties in their smuggling operation, the center of which was a depressed-looking brown bear.

"You'd be depressed too," a tall Romanian told me as he dripped grease from a slab of bacon onto a chunk of bread, "if you'd seen the one creature you adored in your short life, the center of your existence ever since you came into the world—I mean, of course, your mother—shot one day while she was picking berries with you in a meadow, then watched her flayed before your very eyes as you were stuffed into a tiny cage, then forced to witness her killers eat her steaming liver. And if that wasn't enough for a poor outlook on life, how about sleeping in one's own filth, being half-starved, beaten with broomsticks, doused with water, frightened by fire-crackers, and tormented by small children at village fairs until at last a group of gypsies striving to better their lives by becoming international drug smugglers purchased you, and once a month stuffed as many kilos of heroin (safely wrapped in plastic bags, naturally) into your stomach until you had crossed several borders, then were given a diarrhea-inducing root until the bags had all been completely recovered? I don't guess you'd be in such high spirits, either."

It was, of course, merely a coincidence that his hair, even though dull and falling out, was the exact same color and texture as mine, but out of less are stronger relationships forged, and in my case, as two strangers on a train who discover quite by accident a common trait or history, our shared hispidity created an instant bond.

"Tibor," I would say as I passed his cage, "how goes it, brother?" But the bear would merely pace from side to side and grunt with increasingly unpleasant breath. He was a thin bear, and his eyes were red. Perhaps, I thought, he had something stuck in his teeth.

"What have you been feeding this bear?" I asked, and immediately set about to supplement his diet with fresh meat, fruit and vegetables. The results, combined with the attention I gave to his grooming (it turned out he had an abscess on his lower gum), were remarkable. His breath sweetened, his coat gleamed, and while a melancholy nature seemed to be an unchangeable part of his personality, at times I would catch him waving halfheartedly as I walked by. Inevitably, my job consisted of forcing him to swallow his cargo of narcotics (we did this by means of a large rubber dental dam, so his teeth would not puncture the plastic wrapper of each bag) as well as retrieving the bags once we had crossed the border, but even that latter unenviable job, when done in the spirit of brotherhood and interspecies love, was less onerous to me than my callous fellow smugglers could ever have imagined.

Still, life takes strange turns, even for gypsies, and one day one of our members, Andre, came upon a pamphlet written by an American evangelist which described a program, evidently quite well known in that land, called Teen Challenge. In this pamphlet, the Reverend Tony Alamo described the workings of Satan here on earth, and explained that Satan advanced his evil agenda through drugs. It was the existence of heroin, he said, that allowed people to take the easy step to marijuana, and from there to heavy petting, promiscuity, and liberal social programs. Armageddon was coming soon, the Reverend Alamo said, and it was time to stand and be counted. Needless to say, these words soon were transformed into the subject of a fierce debate within the gypsy camp. Each evening after dinner the group seemed to divide into shifting factions, some scoffing at the Reverend's apocalyptic words, while others took the position that one couldn't be too careful. At last, after a week of such debate, by means of the democratic process and freely held elections, we took the twenty or so bags of heroin we were preparing to ship to the American market (home of Tony Alamo himself!) and, digging a deep hole behind a two-star restaurant outside Paris, buried the drugs where no teenagers would ever find them. We resolved to tell the thugs and criminals waiting to pick up their shipment that their "horse" had gotten lost somewhere. "They would," Andre said, "simply have to understand."

VII. Ooglik

Curiously, my creative endeavors on Devil's Island allowed me not only to collect a small but devoted group of fans for my canvases, but also to plan my escape. My situation was this: 1) I could stay or leave. 2) If I left, I could either swim out toward a landless horizon in shark-infested waters, or use a boat. 3) If I chose a boat, I could either obtain one by attempting to overpower a guard and perhaps failing, or use my free time to make one of my own.

So in the end, my art became the means of my escape. The vegetation of the island was thin and generally insubstantial, with few plants larger than a stalk of sugarcane, and certainly none that I could use for planks to make a boat. But at last I came up with a plan. Because of the high prices my work currently was fetching, I was allowed to go to paint each day in a quiet cove on the far side of the island. There, I reasoned, on the pretext of stretching canvases, I could make a craft that resembled a kayak. I was currently working on a group of paintings that had proved to be enormously successful back in Paris, a series I called *Who Is Free Now?* which consisted of a variety of humans, all in cages, being watched by animals who were the keepers.

Thus, like the ancient Chinese artist who walked to freedom through a door he had painted on the canvas before him, I paddled free from my prison. Unfortunately, like him as well, I had not thought through the provision business all that well. I had a couple of baguettes, about a liter of decent Chablis, and a few liters of mineral water, all of which I finished during my first days at sea. The tropical sun beat down, I could feel the scraping of sharks along the bottom of my craft, large birds swooped down to peck at my eyes, and worse, I couldn't seem to get the voice of Edith Piaf out of my mind. Time passed. I woke, I slept, I dreamt, until one state blended into another. I saw my mother and father at a little table of ice, sitting down to a meal of seal—the famine over; I saw Jesus; I saw Paris, Bucharest, Los Angeles, the pyramids along the Nile, and then, looking up, I saw yet another ark, this one even larger than the first, one which carried all the dead from this time backward, ferrying men in the armor of Crusaders and men wearing the liveries of the dynasties of ancient China, cowboys and pharmacists and sportsmen and nurses, the heroes of the *Iliad* and those of ancient Babylon. I saw our earliest ancestors, barely out of caves, still wearing the stinky skins of animals and clutching their crude stone axes, and behind them figures of an even earlier age, various prehuman forms half hidden in shadows, shy and tiny in the presence of all their children and their children's children, as silently, slowly, hugely this great ship stopped for me, and, lowering a thick line over its side, took me on board to where its captain, a dark figure in a hooded cloak, stood, and asked me if my pain had disappeared. I told him yes it had, and it was the first time ever.

VIII. Marnie

What is it like, you ask, you who do not know the power locked within your question, to lose a child you love? As if I can ever describe what it is to see your own self, once single, doubled, and then to see that double grow, venturing out to become a little independent self, to grow more, to develop mutual complaints, phobias, pet names, to watch it begin to take its place in a hostile world and then, without warning or preparation (but what kind of preparation could be adequate for this?), to have it suddenly removed, a thing which *was*, suddenly *not there*, all its feelings and memories irretrievable, an empty space where something had been, a book left open on the eve of a disaster, except that we are the readers, so it is we who are left, it is we who are the repository for missing hope, for missing dreams, for missing pages... what am I supposed to answer?

Such were the thoughts racing through my mind as the grey-haired, professionally dressed agent from Interpol sat on my rustic couch, reporting the death of the man I had come to know as Little Man. He had had few possessions, the man told me, and had left me nothing except—absurdly—a medium-size brown bear, which I promptly donated to a scientific organization where, I was promised, it would be cared for.

In the days that followed, what could I do but weep, and at the strangest moments: seeing lovers nuzzling their innocent noses, holding hands, pushing into phone booths so as not to become separated, and inevitably during that same act Little Man and I had performed so many times ourselves, the act of love. These latter outbursts, because they were business related, were initially a concern to me, but after seeing the salutary effect they had on many (but not all) of my customers, I quickly learned they were an attraction in themselves. I soon developed a reputation as a specialist. Tragically, my business prospered.

Then, one day in the midst of doing "The Bumblebee's Adventure" with a Belgian client, I stopped crying. He was very understanding, and after negotiating a reduction in my fee, wished me happiness, an ironic prophecy, as it turned out, considering the life that followed. My having lost my trademark tears, my old customers soon went elsewhere, and I was reduced to the novice ranks of my profession, the equivalent of a star having to return to the chorus line. To supplement my falling self-esteem, I found myself, almost without noticing, taking small items I hadn't paid for home from stores, and even when I became aware of the situation I did not seem to be able to stop. At last, one day in a fancy department store, a two-pound can of truffles tucked under my arm, I paused to shake the hand of the security guard, an old customer of mine, and the can clattered to the floor. The guard, hypocrite that he was, instantly pretended not to know me, and in the ensuing struggle to make my arrest, his gun (as in our earlier encounters) went off too early. He fell to the marble floor, mortally wounded. I was arrested for his murder, and after a brief trial, sent to She-Devil's Island.

Yes, She-Devil's Island, one of the most infamous correctional institutions in all of France, had been modeled after its patriarchal predecessor, and differed in only two ways. First, it was reserved for women inmates, and second, it was located within the territorial boundaries of France itself, a former castle on an island in the middle of the Rhone rebuilt to contain vixens, hussies, wenches, harpies, witches, broads, molls, hellcats, viragos, spitfires, dykes, bitches, cunts, tarts, shrews, scolds and nags, in short, every woman who at one time or another chose to relinquish the role of victim, and now was paying for it.

Each cell (as the result of a curious gift from a philanthropic female who believed that putting each prisoner in touch with her past life would ameliorate the tedium of incarceration) was designed in the style of a different period in history, and ranged from medieval dungeons to Roman vaults to Asian "Tiger Cages." I chose for myself an early American stockade—simple wooden logs, a rough-hewn bench, and real dirt floors.

In no time at all the women in my cell block—Carmen, Magda, Jeanne, Lucy and Phyllis—became my friends, particularly Lucy, who had had a solid career as a movie star, then married a musician and went on to star in a popular television series in the 1950s before she wound up at She-Devil's Island. "What happened?" I asked her on my arrival. "If you, with all your money and influence and power, could wind up in a place such as this, how can an ordinary woman such as I blame herself?"

"It's clear that you should not," she said, and went on to explain that her downfall began while she was on a visit to France.

"I was vacationing in a fashionable Parisian hotel," Lucy explained, "and happened to notice that staying on the floor beneath me was one of my favorite writers of all time—an obscure American author whose short stories and novellas, as improbable as they sometimes seemed, mirrored perfectly the confusion, tragedy and lack of real identity I felt in my own life. I introduced myself to him. He was gracious and affable, but was embarrassed by the idea of signing books or autographs. He said he was sorry, but would have to deny me my request. A look of anguish passed over his weary face (for he was not a young man), and he backed, still nodding, into an open elevator.

"I don't know why," she said. "Maybe it was because I was not used to being denied my wishes, or maybe it was just because I had signed so many autographs myself, but that moment something snapped. I simply had to have his signature, if only to redeem all those duplicates of my own self I'd handed out so thoughtlessly.

"I decided that if I couldn't get one directly then I would trick it out of him. I dressed up as a waiter, and when he signed the check, I thought I would have my prize. But he kept looking at me strangely during his dinner and paid with cash, leaving behind what would have been, had I been the real item, a surprisingly inadequate tip. Next I dressed as a chambermaid, and climbed into his room through the balcony in the hope I might find a spare signature lying around somewhere, but instead, somehow, while in the process of replacing the sanitized cover of his toilet, I managed to stop the whole thing up. The people on the floor below called the real chambermaids, and I had to flee.

"The next day I returned, disguised as a nun, only to be confronted, in the elevator on the way to his room, by another nun, who was really a man in disguise, a terrorist on a mission to assassinate the ambassador of a foreign government also staying at the hotel. Seeing me in a nun's habit, he mistook me for an accomplice, and tossed me an automatic weapon, so that just as the doors of the elevator opened we found ourselves surrounded by dozens of *gendarmes* and their guns. My companion began to fire, and, because the police were firing their own weapons at me, I felt I had no choice but to join him. Unfortunately, during one of my many tours of troops during the Second World War, I had been given small arms training, and buried as it must have been in some latent memory, it proved much too thorough. I wound up killing a half dozen policemen as well as the ambassador himself, a short man with a mustache and a striped coat who bled to death on the floor at my feet. The terrorist, as it turned out, had been wiped out in the first volley.

"Needless to say, the government was determined to make an example out of me, and so here I am today, along with you, on She-Devil's Island." Lucy sighed, and stood a little straighter. "And even though I am, as you know, completely innocent of all charges, I must say I am proud to take my place along with you and all my less fortunate sisters."

Such, as a matter of fact, were all our sentiments, which is why, at first, the idea of a jailbreak seemed nothing more than an extended diversion to pass the time. But I watched it gradually evolve from a fantasy into a full-blown political statement, or, as Eve, a woman who herself had recently hacked through, as the newspapers phrased it, "a wall of living flesh," put it, "It's an issue of respect. As long as they are sure we won't try anything, they'll just keep taking advantage."

The break was planned during the prison's annual depiction of *The Carnival of the Animals*, a tribute to the composer who had penned this graceful classic work in one of the very rooms of our prison previous to its being turned into a penitentiary. As one might guess, *The Carnival* consisted of the guards dressing in costumes of the swans, fish, lions, and other animals originally included in the musical composition. The rest of us, the prisoners, who wore costumes of sad crustaceans, dejected bears, snakes, lemurs and paramecia—those who had been deemed unworthy to be included—looked on. This time however, as those privileged insiders danced to the music of Saint-Saëns, we the outsiders would create a larger and larger disturbance, until at last, when the music came to an end, those of us left out would completely overwhelm the rest.

The evening came at last. One by one, Saint-Saëns' chosen animals wandered on and off our makeshift stage, their footsteps accompanied by the sound of the rain on the roof, and little by little the disorder spread, engulfing the guards so gradually they didn't notice that the entire prison staff had been taken out of commission until it was too late. (I myself, in the costume of a horned owl, overpowered and tied up two swans on my own.) Finally, when it was clear that we had succeeded beyond our wildest dreams, we prepared to cross the narrow bridge leading from the prison back to the world.

Alas, such an uncomplicated victory was not to be ours. The rain we had been hearing throughout our performance (and which Lucy, with her show business background, had mistaken for distant applause) turned out to be the country's worst torrential storm in living memory. Not only had the bridge been washed away, but the rising water tore at the very foundation stones of our prison. Suddenly what had been our place of confinement was our only hope for safety. What had been a question of freedom became one of life and death itself.

So there we were, having abandoned the guards to their fate, a whole prison full of liberated female criminals in animal costumes, desperately climbing higher and higher to escape the rising flood until, reaching the roof of the old castle, we could go no higher, the stones beneath us trembling against the force of the rushing water, our fur matted and our feathers drooping, when, in what was to be our last sight on earth, we watched horrified as through the torrent an enormous ship, a moving wall of lights, bore down on us at tremendous speed.

IX. Tibor

Who among us can predict, among the thousands of sperm that swim along so blindly searching for an egg, what the product of the eventual union will be like? And who can predict which, out of the myriad witnesses to our lives, will be the one to pass our stories on? Not you, and not the actors of this brief narrative, and certainly not me, an elderly bear, trained by well-meaning scientists to operate a typewriter. Someone, an author once said, always survives to tell every story. Who could have predicted that someone as humble as myself, whose beginnings (early loss of parent, imprisonment, malnutrition and abuse) were so inauspicious, whose wanderings (Bucharest to Paris, Paris to America) were so extensive, whose diet (slop and heroin) was so unpromising, should be the one to write this chronicle.

The dead lie all about me—Little Man, Marnie, Ooglik, even Andre, who had been born again in Jesus just in time to be gunned down in a hail of bullets. Yet, in the words of Samuel Butler, "a hen is just an egg's way of making another egg," and though I can well believe that each of the persons in this tale would no doubt wish for some other, some more dramatic or more witty narrator than a medium-size brown bear to be the repositiory of their brief and lonely stories of their time on earth, nonetheless it pleases me to think that *were* they actually able to return from whatever afterlife they're experiencing, they would agree at least that I have tried to be fair. So I pass on their names and their stories, as you will pass on the names and stories of others. There was a Tibor before me and will be one afterwards, and who is to say where one name, or one being, leaves off and another begins? Each, I like to think, does honor to the others. And if, for that matter, we tell another's story, or someone tells ours, aren't they really just parts of the same? Doesn't the existence of any one part imply the others?

As for me, I'm getting older. Though the cages here at the National Institute of Animal Narrative are clean, they are, regrettably, still cages. I confess that lately I've been having dreams of being free again, of the days before the hunters killed my mother. When I ask my trainers if I'll be released some day, they say of course, but when I ask how soon, they change the subject, so I think I understand. Right now, I'm their prize student, and also they're not sure what would happen to me (or them) if I left to return to "the wild," as they call it.

And concerning those parts of my own life you haven't yet heard, those words not yet impressed by my huge paws upon the oversize keyboard connected to the computer in the adjoining room, what can I tell you that you need to know? There was, or soon will be, a flood. Crimes were and were not committed. We escaped, or did not, from our prisons. We grew old. We wished to pull irretrievable moments from the trash heaps of our memories. We wanted others to have them. We thought they were of value. We died.